MARSHMALLOW TOMBSTONES:
TERRORISM AT 32 DEGREES F

By Eugene (Gene) A. Ritz©

ISBN-13: 978-0-615-57302-1

ISBN-10: 0615573029

This book is dedicated to the late Bill Simunick. His humorous antics, good nature, and love of snowmobiling provided memorable times for this author and many others.

Our "foul weather friend" Bill is still missed on the trails.

ACKNOWLEDGMENTS

I would like to thank the men and women in uniform who have helped maintain our freedoms, enabling us to continue to enjoy this great country as we do. Your sacrifices are truly heroic.

Thanks also to my wonderful wife, Diana, for supporting what has turned into a very long-term effort on my part, to play out to fruition. Many hours on the computer gave us both more time apart than we needed or wanted. She was always willing to make helpful suggestions if asked, but never offered them unsolicited. Extremely capable on a snowmobile in her own right, she has been my partner on the snow for almost forty years since our winter honeymoon in 1971.

Good friends Rich, Ruth, Lisa, Dayle, George, Laura, Mary Ann, and Jan spent time offering suggestions as well as correcting typographical and technical mistakes in the very early drafts. Paulette Bethel of ProEditingService completed the professional editing in fine fashion. Thanks to all of you!

And lastly, a huge 'thank you' to all those tireless, hard working volunteers and snowmobile club members in Canada and the northeastern snow-belt states of Pennsylvania and New York. The trails have never been better, smoother or safer due to your fantastic efforts!

About the Author

Gene A. Ritz, M.Ed. is a retired Technology Education teacher of 35 years and lives with his wife in Pennsylvania. He is intrigued by all things mechanical and holds a United States Utility Patent. He has been a long time member of a local sports car club, as well as several snowmobile clubs, and has always been interested in any and all forms of motor sports. He has owned and restored various rare sports cars.

He and his wife, Diana, first rode snowmobiles in 1971 during their honeymoon at a mountain resort in western Pennsylvania. Since the late 1970's they have been avid snowmobilers riding every winter there is enough snowfall, and traveling to other northern states and Canada in pursuit of the "perfect" snowmobile ride. They often rode with friends in the beautiful southwestern New York region of Chautauqua County. The cover photograph was taken by Gene in that region.

Gene has written numerous articles for a professional technology education magazine in the past, but this is his first novel. Even with the alarming scenario in this work, it is his desire that when reading the vivid descriptions of the beautiful snow covered surroundings found on even a *typical* snowmobile ride, others will get out and enjoy the activity as he, his wife, and many of their friends have. It offers unequaled adventure, excitement and family fun; especially without the terrorists.

TABLE OF CONTENTS

Introduction

As the prolonged Iraq war drew to a close, United States troops returned in more significant numbers to their lives 'back home.' For some, it would be a relatively easy adjustment. For others it would stand as one of the most difficult times of their lives. Special Forces Ranger, Shawn Kaan, made it back without physical scars and almost immediately set about normalizing his life; planning all of the fun filled, interesting, and typically "American" activities available in this great county.

He did however, have a few emotional scars—as might be expected working and living in a war zone for nearly two years—but it was another problem that actually troubled him even more. Shawn was an especially dedicated soldier and was held in very high esteem by his superiors. That is why it struck him so hard when he was asked to leave his unit before his tour was officially over. Although bitter at being given no reason for the early termination, Shawn was unflagging in his loyalty to the military cause. Although he sought answers, none were forthcoming. Now at home, he had a renewed appreciation of life, and he was determined to live it, with or without a positive relationship with the Army.

His hobby of choice was snowmobiling and a major trip was the first item on the "to-do" list when he arrived home in snow covered, rural Pennsylvania. Although thoughts of Iraq and what he had seen and lived through plagued him daily, he loved snowmobiling so much he was able to store most of it in the back of his mind and get out and enjoy what Mother Nature had to offer. His local snowmobile dealer, Jay Shamal, insisted Shawn use a very expensive machine on the trip—as a special favor to him. It was not until the end of the ride that Shawn understood why.

It was on this thrilling trip—the first snowmobile get-away—that Shawn and his wife, Amy, would uncover the real reason he was no longer in Iraq. Unexpectedly their vacation was a working one—one they would never be able to forget!

DREAM LAND

Shawn attempted to nip the apex of the sparkling, ice-encrusted bend to the left. He was pegging at about 30 miles per hour and the weight bias shifted to the right with the sound of breaking glass. One ski broke through the thick, frozen shell that covered the wide field and shards of sparkling, glass-like fragments sailed through the air. His snowmobile dug into the softer snow below and took a sudden pitch, tilting steeply to the right.

Shawn was again caught unawares. He had been daydreaming about how much small crystals of ice looked like white sand. Once sent to the desert, he wondered if would he ever get to see snow again…or was he just going to die somewhere on the sands of Iraq?

He was an inexperienced rider and it was all he could do to hold onto the handlebars. He twisted hard to the right to counter the sudden lurch and then quickly back to the left. He remembered to lean into the turn and forced his butt completely off the left side of the seat and down toward his foot for weight transfer. Shawn, at barely six foot and weighing a mere one hundred and fifty pounds, had trouble wresting the cumbrous mass of the hurtling five hundred pound snowmobile back to center.

Amy, Shawn's girl friend, riding on the seat behind him, was also caught off-guard by the quickness of the event. She tried to react, but didn't have enough time to grab the plastic grip Shawn had installed the week before. She flew off the right side of the snowmobile and hit the frozen surface hard with her head, her right shoulder, and then her back.

Shawn was struggling to keep the sled upright and didn't see Amy leave the seat but he could feel a change through the steering bars and knew weight on the snowmobile had diminished. The reduced weight helped restore the balance and he was able to regain control and complete the turn without rolling the sled over.

Amy wound up on her back and spun by Shawn as he struggled to get the snowmobile to a complete stop. He gaped at her as she continued to spin and slide for several more seconds. Her oversized, dark green snowmobile suit didn't provide enough friction to slow her on the hard, glassy surface. With her arms, legs and head off the ice and pointed upward at the azure Pennsylvania sky, Shawn thought she looked like a big green turtle on its back!

Amy finally ended her 'spinning turtle' impersonation about forty feet away from where she had first touched the ice. She was able to dig in the heel of her boot and slowly roll over. She lay gasping on her stomach, struggling to catch her breath.

Shawn's amusement quickly turned to concern as he realized Amy might have hit her head after being thrown from the snowmobile. He jumped off the sled and immediately broke through the thick crust to the deep snow below. Each step sucked away his energy and cost him countless seconds. The glossy shell that had formed from hours of freezing rain the day before caught at the toes of his boots with every step. He managed to pull one leg out only to fall forward, plunge his other leg through into the snow and flounder again. Shawn was huffing and puffing by the time he got close to Amy who was already standing, hands on her hips, her helmet beside her on the glittering snow.

"I want my own!" she shouted and stomped her boot with a crunching sound. "You're not doing that to me again! I want my own sled or I'm not coming out again…Ever! I could've really been hurt, Shawn!"

4

Seeing that Amy was upset, but physically okay, he tried to calm her down by telling her how funny she looked as she went skidding past him. "You looked like a turtle on its back, spinning and sliding, sliding and spinning."

He couldn't keep himself from laughing as he used his hands to pantomime how Amy had looked, much as he did in the classroom when making a point to his students.

That would prove to be his second major mistake of the day as Amy bent down, picked her helmet up by the strap, whirled it once around her head and let it go—directly at Shawn. He turned and tried to run but kept tripping and falling, making no headway for what seemed to be long minutes, the helmet pummeling his back all the while.

As Shawn kicked and struggled, the bed sheets wrapped about his feet momentarily and roused him from his dream-turned-nightmare. He opened his eyes just enough to see the large, digital numbers on the clock in front of him. Amy continued to bump and push on his back urging him to wake up. She finally stopped when he didn't respond. He drifted back into his dream again.

Twenty minutes later the bedroom began to lighten from the rising sun. Amy stirred and punched Shawn again; this time on the shoulder and much harder. She then buried her head under her pillow, holding it around the back of her neck with both hands. Since they have been married, Amy, who was slender and just over five feet tall, found that sometimes she had to exert herself to make a point with Shawn…whack!

"Ouch!" Shawn jerked and then lay still.

She quipped softly, "Quit it, Brad. You've been tossing all night long, keeping me awake. What's the matter, forget to pack something?" she yawned and rolled onto her back.

Shawn, still only half awake said with a moan, "Nah, just dreaming, I guess. Yep, that's all, just a dream... Did you say Brad? Did you just call me... did you just call me Brad?"

His hearing had been damaged from the bombings in Iraq, so he was unsure he had heard her correctly. He yawned, sighed and rubbed his eyes. Slowly, he rolled his lanky, thirty year old body out from under the covers. He perched on the left side of the king-sized bed. Still only half awake he muttered something indiscernible even to himself.

He had not been sleeping well since returning from the war—usually bad memories of Iraq that manifested as nightmares. He admitted it was a tough physical and mental adjustment. He had told Amy he would actually be more comfortable sleeping on their gravel driveway than on the pillow topped bed Amy bought while he was gone. He still didn't know why she bought it. Money had been really tight since the school district stopped the checks last year, and she was sleeping alone.

His eyes snapped open when he remembered he hadn't packed all his clothes for their first big snowmobile trip north into Canada. His concern didn't last more than a few seconds, however, as he remembered what his second dream was about. He closed his eyes once again, slumped on the edge of the bed with a smile on his face, and slowly re-lived the wonder of it.

This dream wasn't about riding with Amy on a snowmobile. It was triggered by his recollection of the day before when he picked up their snowmobiles at *The Sled Shop*. He had found the machine of his dreams… the mother of all high performance sleds.

Jabr Shamal—Jay to the locals—was the shop's owner, a sixty year old, overweight, ex-military man with an attitude more like a native New York cab driver than the Syrian immigrant he was. He was a large man with coal-black, wavy hair and gray stubble on his face. He exhibited an imposing, "in your face" nature. As he stood close beside Shawn he spoke loudly, with a distinct accent; a wet, stubby, unlit cigar clenched in his teeth.

"Yeah, nothin' faster than one o' these new XMZ's," Jay said to Shawn as they both stared at the sled perched on a brightly lighted stand that made it look even more massive than it was.

Shawn mutely stared at the imposing machine.

The snowmobile was a deep black with metallic red and gold flames on its hood and flanks. The vents were large and open, giving it the look of a monster able to inhale as much air as it needed to cool the turbo-charged engine within the cowling. The sculpted bodywork was aerodynamic; the glistening plastic skin stretched tightly over the high tech mechanicals. The windshield, laid back and very low, gave it a rakish appearance that exuded speed even when standing still.

Wow! Shawn thought, as he walked slowly around the machine.

"Fix ya up a real good deal on this baby. Ten big ones and she's yours," Jay said. "It's a rare one. Don't see too many, oh, and damn fast. Worth some major bucks," he added.-

"You've got to be kidding," Shawn responded and then added, "It is beautiful, but who's got the cash for a ten-grand snowmobile?"

"Why…One o' you *independent* government contractors, I suppose," Jay answered. "It's all around. I heard you guys are well paid, sometimes hundreds of thousands a year. Ought'a have this much, no?" He pointed to the sled.

Shawn knew he couldn't say anything about what he did for the Army. He shook his head and grinned.

"Big money, huh? This beauty's not in my garage, is it? Looks to me like its sitting in your nice, big showroom, Jay, along with all of those," he pointed and looked around at several dozen shiny new snowmobiles. "Looks to me like you're the one with all the big money here, Bub!"

Jay Shamal hesitated, and then continued.

"Sold one just like this a couple months ago to Bob, the dentist. Ya know, one o' them what you'd call a '*super* yuppie,' I guess. Anyway, he's got big bucks. So he took it up north and lost it," he chuckled and shook his head in disbelief.

"Lost it! He lost it? How could you lose something like this?" Shawn nodded his head at the exotic machine.

"Well, I guess what really happened was some bad-ass mountain man ripped him off. Up there where you're goin'. Lemme put it this way," Shamal continued, laughing. "Never did find it. But what the hell, insurance company paid 'em fer it. Problem is, Doc had me order this other one here right away. Oh, yeah, had to have it *right away!* And then,

8

after I busted my ass to get it fer him decided he's gonna stick with downhill skiing, after all. Okay with me, though, cause I kept his deposit! Like I said, I'll work a helluva deal for a rich guy like yourself. If ya want her. Just gimme eighty-five hundred and she's yours! That is, of course, with yer ol' one in trade."

"Of course!" said Shawn sarcastically. "Let's see, my old snowmobile is worth about thirty-five hundred. Then lets add the eighty-five hundred you want for this monster...ah, um, ah...yep, yeah, that's just about right. I should've figured you'd want about twelve thousand bucks for a ten thousand dollar sled—*after* you keep the guy's deposit!

"You know, Jay, I know how to do the barter thing, too. But you won't get me to bite, especially for something I don't even need."

Shawn's voice had begun to rise. He stopped speaking and took a calming breath; he realized he must have sounded a lot like Amy to Jay. Jay and Amy got along okay, but she never did feel comfortable talking with him one-on-one because he was always so domineering, loud and abrasive. She described him to others as being a 'simply obnoxious oaf.'

Shawn had always liked Jay because he considered him someone who had real character and because he was of Middle Eastern descent. He understood what immigrants from that region faced when coming here because his dad had faced those same prejudices when he immigrated.

Shawn considered Jay a survivor in a tough, expensive and seasonal business that dealt with primarily white, upper-middle class, often racially-biased Americans. Jay had had some rough years, laced with plenty of discrimination and very little snow. He had endured name calling and broken store windows ever since the first mid-eastern/OPEC oil embargo put a crimp on the recreational industry decades ago. Though bitter at first, Jay still believed America was the land of opportunity. Jay had sponsored other immigrants from various Middle Eastern countries to visit; he had even convinced others to move here.

"Well, suit yourself, then," said Jay as he turned toward the door. He was disappointed that he hadn't been able to strike the deal he thought he had going.

He then surprised Shawn a little when he added, "Someday you'll wish you had a 140 mile per hour sled when that cute little wife of yours decides to take up with a new guy out on the trail or something! And you ain't gonna be able to do jack shit about it, sonny! Not with that ol' tired dog of yours out there. You're being really stupid here!" He pointed through the window at Shawn's sled one of the workers was placing on his trailer.

Shawn was surprised at what Jay had just said to him. He was really startled by Jay's reference to Amy; he didn't think Jay even noticed she was good looking.

"Well, jeez, gimme a break here, buddy," said Shawn. "Even if I could buy something like this, you know I'd be riding the brake all day long so that Amy could keep up. Then you'd be talking her into something way too fast and… well, she'd just hurt herself again!"

Shawn was referring to when they bought Amy's first snowmobile from Jay; before Shawn left for the Army and just after he dumped her onto the ice. On her first ride she rolled it doing hundreds of dollars worth of damage. The accident occurred when she missed a sharp curve and slid sideways, catching the drive belt in a rut.

The sled flipped over and had gone airborne. When Shawn got turned around and came back, he was terrified to see Amy lying there, not moving, looking like she was dead, half buried in soft snow.

She got up very slowly from that one. They realized how lucky she was when they noticed the sled had to have traveled at least thirty feet in the air past where Amy had landed. She was shaken up and bruised, but very fortunate. She managed to ride the badly damaged sled back to the hotel where they were staying.

Shawn was afraid that Amy wouldn't want to ride anymore after her accident. But within just a few weeks, she was once again on the trails with him. Amy, who initially had been a very cautious rider, now had a tendency to overdrive her machine, almost as if she needed to prove she could handle the rough terrain and dangerous curves.

However, it was the main reason Amy didn't like Jay. They all knew he had failed to check the suspension on Amy's snowmobile when he sold it to her and she blamed him for the accident. He made excuses for his ineptness and it left a sour taste in Amy's mouth. She didn't trust him.

"Well, you owe me for fixin' up the hunk o' junk you ride. It'll be four fifty," Jay interjected, ending Shawn's thoughts of the early sled riding days. "I ain't got time to piss with a rich government contractor with too much money and no brains here!"

"Man, Jay, your killing me. All you did was a couple quick tune-ups and new wear bars and it's almost five hundred bucks? Are you *serious*?" Shawn was getting pissed, too.

"Awe, don't start whining here. Let the little guy make a few bucks once in awhile, huh?" said Jay. He paused for a few seconds as if deep in thought and then said, "Alright then, if you're gonna be a frog's ass about it. Three hundred even. And just forget about that sweet deal on the XMZ!"

Shawn knew full well the inflated repair bill stemmed from Jay's roots and always occurred when dealing with him about anything that was done to the snowmobiles. He pulled three one hundred dollar bills from his wallet.

Shawn handed Jay the money and said, "Sounds better. I don't have the funds to take you up on your offer for that new one. I'd have to sell my old 'Vette, and you know I've had that car for ten years now."

"You're breakin' my heart here. Pay up an' lemme get back to makin' some *real* money since I can't make any on you." Jay grumbled as he pulled the cash from Shawn's hand.

Then Jay added, "Uh, seriously, Shawn, if ya see Doc's XMZ up north when you're ridin', gimme a cell buzz—real quick. Insurance company might work another deal on it... or," pausing, "I'd just re-sell it! Can't say nutin' to nobody, though, got it? Got it? I'll cut ya in for a few hundred if ya do. 'Member, though, between me an you, no one else! Not even your cutie-pie wife. Do it, look fer it and gimme a call when you find it and tell me exactly where you are."

"Ah, oh, yeah, sure Jay, I'll do that, no problem," Shawn said as he counted the remaining cash in his wallet.

Shawn left the shop and quickly checked the tie-downs before he climbed into the Jeep. As he turned the ignition key, he pondered why Shamal was so insistent that Shawn look for the missing sled. If Shawn participated in

12

some insurance deal, wouldn't that be some kind of fraud? Probably not, he would just be helping the company get the sled back; in fact, they would probably be happy to get it back.

Why even think about it? Jay implied he would come and get the lost snowmobile since he wanted to know the exact location of the find. It was a huge area, odds were he'd never come across that sled. Shawn put the selector into drive and pushed the tow mode button on the dash

As he started to drive away he heard a muffled cry from behind him.

"Hey, Shawn... Shawn," Jay yelled from the garage door opening. "Wait... come on back in here."

Shawn stopped and put the Jeep into park. He let it idle and walked back to the shop door that Jay held open for him.

Shamal put his hand out to Shawn for a shake.

"Listen, you've been a really, really good customer of mine for a long time. I feel bad about yelling at you. I made a 'not so nice' comment about your beautiful wife. I know you give a lot to your country. You're a patriot, I respect that. I think a lot of that, I really do. I give back to my country, as well. You don't know! I don't want you mad at me. So I have an idea... You like that big sled a lot, no? You really, really like it, right? No?"

Shawn, puzzled, slowly shook Jay's hand and said with a shrug, "No problem, Jay...I...I'm ok. I'm not angry or anything. Don't worry about it, it's all right."

"No, no, I'm going to do a real good thing here. I insist," Jay pointed at Shawn's trailer and nodded at one of his mechanics. "It will heal my honor. You take my new XMZ

13

for a nice long ride this week, uh? You break her in *good* for me, no? She'll run like hell for you. Much faster than your old tired dog there. Right?"

"I…I can't do that, Jay. It's not right. I know I can't buy it. It'd be wrong to take it. What if something happened to it? I couldn't pay you for it. No, no…I better not, Jay. And really, it's okay."

"No, Jay won't take no!" Jay said loudly, as the worker quickly finished un-strapping Shawn's old sled. "Don't humiliate me! I want this to be!"

The XMZ appeared on a dolly in the doorway. Shawn stopped resisting. There was a sparkle in his eye.

"I…I shouldn't, Jay, really. You know, but, um…Well, hmm, boy, it sure would be a sweet experience, huh? I mean, I'd probably never get a chance to ride one like that! Are you sure? You think it'd be okay?"

Jay backed through the door and smiled as he said, "Not just for anyone. Just you, Shawn. You're an Arab brother. We're all in this together. You're helping me out here, really. You don't know how much. All controls are the same, okay? Only thing different is pull start. High compression, too. You'll bust your ass startin' her but then hang on. You'll see. Call when you're done with her."

The door closed with a thud.

Walt, the mechanic, finished loading the XMZ and told Shawn his old sled would be covered and stored outside. He also showed Shawn where the fuel shut off was on the XMZ since he would trailer it a long distance. He paused when he was done and looked Shawn in the eye.

He said seriously, "Be very careful Shawn. Stay alert. Keep your eyes open."

"No problem, Walt. You know how I ride." Shawn said in a puzzled way.

Shawn thanked him and climbed into the Jeep. He couldn't believe what had just happened. It took him a few seconds and then he pulled slowly out of the driveway. He thought to himself that Jay had never been this generous before. He couldn't figure out why Jay would do this. Maybe it was just as Jay had said. He was proud that Shawn served his country. Maybe that struck a chord with him since Jay had been in the Syrian military.

Right now, Shawn got to ride the sled. To hell with why it happened!

"Hey! Hey! Hey!"

Now what, Jay? Lemme guess, you changed your mind? Shawn thought to himself.

But this time, the voice wasn't Jay's. It was Amy and Shawn's reflections on dream number two were over.

She yelled over her shoulder as she headed toward the bathroom.

"Hey, Shawn, gonna get up sometime today? You gonna finish packing or what? I told you the last time I wasn't going to do all the packing again! You'd better get your butt in gear, bucco. We've got a long drive today before we even get close to the trails. We're supposed to leave early. You gonna make me act like your Major, here?"

Only silence from Shawn as he slowly stood up and smiled.

Louder, she appeared in the doorway and shouted into the bedroom. "Let's go, Speed-o! Move it! If you're not fast enough for me, I'll...I'll go without you and find some guy

15

who is and then you'll be sorry. I'm taking a quick shower so get up and get the rest of your stuff together! Now! Do it now, Shawn!"

Shawn rubbed his face and said quietly, "Fast enough? Nothin's faster than my new sled."

"I heard that. A new sled? Maybe in your dreams, champ!"

"Oh yeah. In my dreams," mumbled Shawn as he made his way to the front of the house and the old bathroom.

He talked louder as he walked by the bathroom that Amy was in.

"Maybe I'll just dump my old car and get a new sled. A really fast one. Shamal has a great deal on one... Did you say Brad? Did you call me Brad, before?"

Amy poked her head out of the shower as steam swirled around her.

"If you remember, Shawn, you always say you want to sell your car in the winter and get a new 'super' sled. And then, in the spring, for some reason, you always want to sell the sled to buy another, faster car. You should have thought of that before you stored it and enlisted. I could've used the car money for bills! You can't have everything, ya know. Come on, now, move your butt and let's get ready. And no, I said 'Babe.' It's those ears, Shawn. Better get 'em fixed before the Army screws you out of that money, too!"

"Yeah, yeah," he sighed and continued shuffling slowly along the hardwood floors headed for the other shower.

Shawn made a decision; he would not tell her the 'real deal' with Jay and the XMZ, at least not for a while. He

16

would fill her in after she saw it. It would be hilarious. *It would teach her a lesson*, he thought.

As Shawn turned on the shower he thought, *I bet I could get at least a thousand bucks for that antique tractor. I could sell a bunch of the other collectible Corvette stuff. I bet I could buy it and keep the car, too.* The sled was a real deal after all.

Once in the hot shower, though, Shawn realized he had two chances of actually buying the new sled: *slim and none.* He rationalized that since he had a good—albeit older—snowmobile, a decent classic Corvette and an adequate tow vehicle, *enough toys already*! Amy was right. He should be happy. With his pending military pay added to his teaching salary, he and Amy would be in good financial shape. They both had good careers and a nice home in the country. There, done, out of his thoughts… at least for a while. Even though he knew he couldn't afford to buy that monster sled, he would get to run it this week. That was the good thing.

He dried off, shook his head and thought to himself, *I wonder if that thing can really hit 140 like Jay claims.* Then, smiling, he said out loud, "Wow, 140! Sweet!"

PREPARATION AND PLANS

Each year when the weather got colder and the first flurries were seen in November and December, Amy and Shawn spent a lot of time on the computer and the weather channel checking both local and national weather. They were watching for trends that indicated when and where the snow would fall. Many times they had experienced local spring-like weather only to find plenty of snow in the higher elevations.

The weather report for their first long get-away was not the greatest; there seemed to be a consensus among most of the weather prognosticators that there was only a very slight chance of a large, low pressure area arriving off the coast, bringing with it an anticipated snowstorm event. They just hoped there would be enough existing snow to ride on once they got to their destination.

This trip would be special. It was supposed to be an escape from all that had happened with Shawn and the military and a celebration of his return to doing what he really loved: teaching. It would take them farther north, actually into Canada, and promised to bring even more exciting riding than their usual destinations in upstate and western New York.

It meant they would have to tow the snowmobiles at least a day, but they intended to break that up with an intermediate ride before reaching their final destination. They planned to bring extra cans of gasoline. Shawn thought the gas would be a drain on their limited space and resisted the idea but Amy was adamant.

Normally they would lay out a route that included trailside fuel stops but they expected to be in unfamiliar country and didn't know how many or even if there would be places to refuel. Snowmobiles, like cars, vary in fuel consumption and capacity and careful planning could mean the difference between having a great time or towing a dry sled for miles. They intended to fill the empty cans at one of their roadside fuel stops prior to their first destination, the trailhead at Wolf Pond, New York.

They planned to travel about six hours to that spectacular area, ride the sleds until just before dark and then refuel and continue on to their destination, a quaint lakeside resort that would be their base for the weekend.

Amy thought this would give them a chance to explore some of the sights she knew they wouldn't stop for on their way back home, break up the tedious drive and refresh their rusty riding skills. They would then be better prepared for the wilderness they intended to penetrate, the rugged Black Caves/Highlands region of Canada. She knew all they would want to do after long days of riding would be to get home and soak in the hot tub before heading back to work.

It was almost time to hit the road and Shawn turned on the computer to do a last minute weather check. The computer was so slow that he decided to dump the old emails that he and Amy had been exchanging for two years and was surprised to find it had already been done. It was unlike Amy to clean up the computer but Shawn didn't think too much about it.

"Got all your stuff, Shawn?" asked Amy as she pointed to Shawn's bulging duffle bag at the front door. "I mean everything? How 'bout toothbrush... sweaters... jeans... extra socks... jocks... silkies...weather radio? Oh, don't put your passport in there. Keep it in the car; we'll have to show it at the border."

"Yep, all done. Packed and, uh, speaking of packed...I'm taking my side arm. Just so you know," he pulled out a holster with a nickel plated .38 in it.

"Better think that one over, Shawn," replied Amy.

"Why? There are wild animals up there you know," Shawn said, with a slight grin on his face.

"I'll say it again, so listen closer this time. You'd better think that one over, Shawn," she suddenly grew serious. "If you get caught with that pistol in Canada it could mean six months in jail. How'd you explain that to your school board? Remember, you're not in the military anymore. Please, leave it here, okay Shawn?"

Shawn moved his head from side to side ever so slightly to signal he was not inclined to agree and continued to bury the gun deeper in his bag.

Knowing Shawn would carry on like this as long as she participated, Amy added, "It's just not worth it, Shawn. I mean, we're crossing the border. They might search the Jeep. They do that sometimes—most of the time, actually. It would be just our luck, ya know? I don't want you to take it. They could confiscate everything. We're just starting to get back to normal. Please, take it out; I don't want it with us!"

"Oh, come on, Amy. I'll hide it in my sled's storage box then. They'd never look in there, not in a million years. You know how I am about going to a strange place in the wilderness without it. I mean you never know... *You know*?

I'm licensed to carry it, at least in this country. That should count for something," Shawn's voice trailed off.

Amy pointed her finger directly at Shawn's face. "I'm serious, Shawn. I want it outta there or I'm not going! I can think of better ways to spend the next six months than in a Canadian prison. Just for being safe? *Give-me-a- break!* Take it out... *NOW!*"

"Okay... okay, Amy!" Shawn said resignedly, "But don't look to me to fight off a wolf, a bear or anything else if we get in trouble up there! I'm outta there, takin' off and leaving. Don't count on me to stick around if things turn ugly." Shawn still hoped she would relent.

Amy lightened up a little knowing that Shawn realized she was deadly serious about the gun.

"Look, Shawn, the sleds make a lot of noise, right? So what're the chances that a wild animal is going to approach us? Besides, I ride way too fast for some dumb ol' wolf or bear to keep up. You know that, right, bucco?"

Shawn did know that. He shrugged his shoulders and reluctantly took the pistol from his bag, unloaded it, and placed it in the back of the drawer of his nightstand.

Shawn wasn't actually concerned about the possibility of wild animals attacking them. In this time and place, however, he wasn't certain about some of the people they could encounter. Terrorists and other dangerous people frequently crossed the all too vulnerable Canadian/U.S. border. He had heard stories from others and would rather have some kind of equalizer if the need arose.

It was his idea to go on this snowmobile trip in the first place so he felt responsible for Amy's well being on the trails. If the need arose, he could do that better with a side-arm. To him it was a question of necessity; good insurance.

He thought about the argument and shuddered at the thought of what a felony gun conviction would mean to his teaching career. He would be finished. And there was his income to consider, his military pay would never cover the loss in income, *if he ever got it.* For some reason, the government had been dragging their feet on settling up what he would be getting; anything negative would only make things worse.

Shawn then recalled one of his fellow teachers who had forgotten about a hand gun he put in his book bag after target practice. He ended up losing his carry permit and was suspended from teaching for a year. If that was the result of a verifiable, unintended mistake, Shawn couldn't even begin to guess what would happen if he intentionally broke the law.

It was one of the big differences he was struggling to adjust to now that he was back in the states, he mused. In Iraq even children sometimes carried weapons; adult males always. He realized he still had adjustments to make; he needed to forget about events in Iraq.

Shawn was satisfied that he was doing the best thing by leaving the gun at home.

Rolling

With the Jeep packed and ready to go, Amy did a quick walk through to double-check the house. Shawn did a check of his own on the towing equipment.

While Shawn might, at times, overlook a detail or two in his personal life, he always paid special attention to any equipment he was responsible for. It didn't matter if it was as a physics teacher or as a soldier—or anything pertaining to his favorite activity of snowmobiling—anything with even the slightest potential for problems was closely monitored to make absolutely certain everything that could be done was more than adequate to insure a safe event. Shawn never wanted someone else to have to pay for his mistakes.

Amy walked briskly through the kitchen, stopping briefly to set the alarm system. As the alarm consol beeped the final seconds before arming, she reached for the door handle. Just as she opened the door she saw the large brown envelope she had accepted from the delivery service for Shawn the day before. It was lying near the corner of the countertop, far across the room.

She briefly thought about taking it along but decided not to. It was from the Department of Homeland Security and would probably just get Shawn worked up about his situation with the military. They probably wanted him to take a security job at the Mexican border or something. He would turn them down anyway, she surmised. She stepped out and closed the door with a thunk.

They drove slowly out of their private country lane that they shared with nine other households and waved good-bye to one of their early rising neighbors. This time even old Mr. Hawkins smiled and waved back at them with his cell phone as he walked his dog. That was surprising because he usually either turned away or just nodded when he saw them towing their snowmobiles. Amy wasn't sure why he seemingly had a problem with their choice of snowmobiling but he seemed to have turned into a bit of a green activist-tree-hugger type since retiring as the county deputy sheriff. He had also had trouble catching thieves who had used snowmobiles as get-away vehicles after breaking into nearby cabins.

Shawn and Amy's friends who were snowmobile enthusiasts would no more break into a boarded-up cabin than they would a church sanctuary. But they understand that Mr. Hawkins and others had a right to their opinions and there was probably nothing they could say that would change that. They smiled and waved back as they drove slowly by so as not to incense his other major concern in life: speeding!

After a couple of minutes Amy said, "How about old Hawkins. Thought he wasn't waving any more. Surprised me there. Maybe he found out these things don't pollute nowadays."

"Oh, I don't think it's that, Amy."

"You think he's still pissed about you riding illegally that time? That was a long time ago, Shawn."

"Could be, Amy. He should be thankful I made it easy for him, huh?"

"Well, duh...yeah."

"I'm just glad we have places to ride where we're welcome, ya know? Places that have trails to support the sport. And places that count on the income in the winter. It's so different than when we first rode around here."

"I'll say, Shawn."

Five winters ago, on a Saturday evening after a rare two foot snowfall unexpectedly fell, Shawn's neighbor, Bob, called and asked Shawn to take him riding around their neighborhood. At that time Shawn and Amy had only ridden in farm fields and on their friends' property; they weren't aware there was a great snowmobile trail system only eighty miles to their north.

"Shawn, what are you doing, buddy?" asked Bob on the phone.

"Watching a game show, you know. Amy likes them. Why?"

"Let's go out on your sleds tonight. We could run up route eight!"

"You think? Oh, I don't know, it's not closed or anything, is it?"

"Hell yeah it is! Didn't you hear?" He was silent for several seconds and then added, "Oh yeah, forgot, you're not watching the news. The governor just declared a state of emergency, man. That means we can use snowmobiles to get around instead of cars. Remember?"

"Oh, yeah? Really? Well, I can go out for a while I guess," Shawn looked at Amy snuggly curled up on the couch. "Amy, interested?"

"I'm not going out there. I'm staying by this fireplace 'til daylight. Then I'll go out. You can go. I don't care," then she added in a whisper so Bob couldn't hear her, "You use my sled. Bob's too big for mine. Let him ride yours."

"Ah, yeah, okay Bob. Let's go out for an hour or so. I'm not saying I'll do route eight though, I'm not sure about that being allowable, but, yeah… Meet me in the barn in ten minutes and bring your motorcycle helmet, Amy's face mask is broken."

"Great!"

"Be careful, Shawn," Amy said, "I don't want you on route eight, though, just ride the fields. Okay?"

"I'm always careful. Did you wash my face mask?"

"Yeah, on the dryer. See ya in about an hour." She stood up and gave him a kiss and then walked toward the bathroom.

"Okay, if I don't go on route eight I might run over toward Mars Borough and see if George is home."

"Whatever. Just watch yourself!"

Bob and Shawn met in the barn and checked the fuel, turned the sleds around, then started them and pulled down the door.

"Wow, I get the big one this time," Bob said with a smile.

"Yeah, not my idea. Amy says your ass is too fat for hers. So I'm stuck on her wimpy one."

"Stick it, Shawn!" Bob said, laughing. "You wanted to come out and play. You know you did. You don't care what you're riding; it's a ride, right? It'll be great!"

"Yeah, this is real deep, though. Not sure how far we'll get in the fields. Careful."

"Always careful, Shawn. You know, since I wrecked mine two years ago, I'm *very* cautious now!"

"Nice, had to remind me, huh?"

They mounted the idling snowmobiles and with Shawn in the lead headed across Bob's back yard toward the farm land they would ride on. The snowmobiles struggled through the heavy wet blanket of snow. Shawn had the throttle almost wide open just to get through some of the drifts they encountered. Shawn figured Amy was right in thinking Bob would have never been able to ride her sled through this stuff tonight. It was way too deep and he was way too heavy.

It took them another five minutes to get to a road crossing. As they approached the road Shawn was thinking, but Bob was planning....

When they hit the road, Bob immediately took a right turn and shot past Shawn. Shawn knew what he was up to and followed.

After cruising down the road for about a mile they came to a stop sign. Posted just above it was a road sign that read: *PA.State Route 8.*

Bob didn't even slow down; he simply merged and accelerated hard, heading north onto the undivided four lane highway... with Shawn in hot pursuit.

The riding surface was perfect and Shawn felt only a little guilty because he knew Amy would be upset if she found out. On the other hand, there were no cars even attempting to traverse the buried highway. Shawn had never seen it this abandoned. There was no one else around, not even a PennDOT truck making a pass with a plow or salt. The road hadn't been touched by any vehicle. *This is awesome*, he thought. He supposed the plows wouldn't be out until Sunday morning and he knew that if the governor had truly declared a state of emergency, it was legal to use snowmobiles on state roads for transportation. He was just not certain it meant *four lane* highways!

They rode up and down the same five mile stretch for about twenty minutes and didn't see anyone else. Shawn, getting bored, remembered he wanted to ride over to the small village of Mars. He recalled many years ago seeing snowmobile signs posted along several back country roads leading right into the heart of town. They could ride over and visit a friend at his farm on the other side of town.

Without stopping to offer an explanation, Shawn passed Bob. He turned west onto the road they came in on and ran up to about fifty miles an hour. Bob's headlight was barely visible through the swirling plumes of snow. It only took them a few minutes at that speed to enter the tiny borough of Mars. It was a blast to ride on roads they had only driven cars on… a totally different experience.

It looked like a Currier and Ives greeting card when they arrived. They saw only a few bundled-up citizens out shoveling sidewalks under the street lights. They entered the quaint village by means of the abandoned railroad tracks and stayed off the main street. It had been plowed and salted.

Shawn missed the turn because he was busy looking at the people who were looking at them. He slowed and tried to make a sweeping turn so he wouldn't have to stop and lift the rear of the sled. He was moving at about five miles an hour when a ski caught an old railroad siding switch and instantly stopped, throwing Shawn over the handlebars.

Bob stopped just in time to keep from running into Shawn or his sled. He sat there laughing along with the village people.

Shawn wasn't hurt and slowly got up and tried to release the ski from the old track switch. He couldn't do it by himself and signaled for Bob to pull on the rear bumper. They struggled for several minutes to release the ski. Shawn didn't take time to inspect for damage. He had attracted the attention of several people from across the sidewalk and was embarrassed by his unexpected dismount. He and Bob made it safely back to the turn and crossed the street, making loud scraping sounds with the skis.

They swung around the small town square that was home for the flying saucer the high school tech class had made and rode out of town as swiftly as they arrived. Shawn had been on this country lane quite a few times but it was a lot prettier at night, in the snow, on snowmobiles.

They rode for several miles and didn't see anyone else. They crested a steep hill and started down the other side when Shawn saw some snowmobile tracks. He followed them as they drifted from one side of the road to the other. When he reached the bottom of the hill, Shawn left the road and ventured onto the field where the other sled had gone. Just as he veered into the open field, Shawn glimpsed a brief sparkle in his headlight. He suddenly realized what it was and turned sharply right, hitting the brakes and broad sliding to a stop.

Bob, again following too close behind, almost hit him. Shawn got off his snowmobile and walked to the spot where he had seen the sparkle only a foot or so away. He was right; his headlight had picked up an ice covered, barbed wire fence that could have decapitated him if he had hit it at speed!

Whew! Shawn said to himself as he walked back to his sled. He just pointed to the fence for Bob to see and got back on his snowmobile. Apparently the snowmobile tracks they had been following were from a local rider who knew to lift the single strand fence before driving under it. *A very close call,* he thought, not one he would tell Amy about. Bob had better not either.

They pulled slowly back onto the road and up another hill, Shawn thinking to himself, *that's how people get killed; doing stupid things on a sled in unfamiliar territory.* He was not pleased with himself and knew Bob would never let him forget this lapse in his normally careful riding style.

Several miles later, almost to their destination, they topped a rise and saw a car about an eighth of a mile away. It was moving slowly in their direction. As Shawn moved to get out of the roadway, he saw red and blue lights come on; it was the police.

Shawn spotted a driveway just in front of them and quickly headed for it. He pulled into the drive and stopped about twenty feet off the road. Bob pulled up next to him and yelled, "What are you doing, Shawn? Go, go! He'll never catch us. Just go! Are you nuts, man?" Bob exclaimed.

The police car was struggling slowly up the hill.

Shawn ignored him and removed his helmet. He watched the patrol car come to a sliding stop on the road and remembered the close call with the fence. He wasn't about to lose his head over some innocuous questions.

The local cop was an older man with dark hair and a matching mustache. He got out of his cruiser and trudged up the snowy driveway, almost falling down on the uneven surface buried beneath the snow; his black brogans barely able to gain any traction

"What the hell do you think you're doing?" he said in a loud and irritable way.

"Riding," Shawn and Bob said in unison, shrugging their shoulders.

"It's just *great* tonight," Shawn added.

"Where the hell are you two from?"

"Oh, uh, from over in Middletown," Shawn said flipping his right hand, thumb extended back over his shoulder indicating where they came from and wondering why this cop was so annoyed.

"What makes you think you can ride here?"

"Well," Shawn said, "I've seen signs on this road that said we could. Besides, there's that state of emergency thing."

"Signs? Signs? On *this* road? I don't think so. Not here. You're dreaming," the cop said pulling out a citation book. "And there is no state of emergency, either!"

"No, really. I saw them. I *know* I saw them," Shawn insisted. "And what do you mean 'no state of emergency'? The Governor declared it." He glanced over at Bob, who avoided eye contact.

"No way," said the cop.

"No, really, sir, I did," Shawn reiterated.

"Well then, tell me when you saw them, these signs?"

"Well, the last time I drove over here in the winter. When there was a lot of snow on the ground. They had the signs posted. I'm *sure* it was on this road. My friend George lives right down there." Shawn was really trying to be reasonable.

Bob stood by silently. So far he hadn't contributed anything to the conversation.

"Well, I'll tell you something. We haven't had those signs up for ten years!" said the officer.

Shawn thought for a moment and then said with a smile, "Yep, you're right, officer. That was the last time we had snow around here, ten years ago." He grinned and looked over at Bob who was slowly shaking his head.

"That's it." the cop said quickly, "Gimme your licenses and insurance cards."

"Oh, come on, officer," Bob finally said. "We're not teenagers or kids here. We're adults. And we stopped right away. We're not doing anything dangerous. We weren't speeding or anything. We didn't know we weren't allowed. He thought he heard about a state of emergency. He got some bad information. Ask the President; it happens. How about letting us off with a warning? We'll leave. We'll just go back home, carefully. No problems. Okay?"

"And just how are you going to *get* home?" the cop asked.

Shawn said, "We'll go back the same way we came in. Back the same roads."

"No, no way." stated the cop. "I can't allow that. You'll have to get a trailer, trailer them back. And don't ever come over here again like this!"

Shawn thought this guy was on a power trip and figured he would be writing them a ticket, anyway. Maybe Shawn should put in his two cents worth.

"Look, ah, Sir. You're asking us to take a risk, a *big* risk. My wife has never towed a trailer before. She is going to have to come over here on your unplowed roads to get to us. Do you really think that is better than just letting us ride back the way we came? I don't mind saying, I think *that* would be irresponsible right there, sir. And if there's a wreck...well..."

The cop just stared at Shawn. "You may have a point. But, like I said, don't ever do this again. You won't get off so easy next time!"

"You bet! Thanks!" said Shawn smiling. " And we'll stay on the edge of the road, close to the guardrail, okay?"

"Yeah, yeah. Just get out of here."

"Yes, sir. Have a nice night," Bob chimed in.

The cop said nothing more, just turned and carefully walked down the driveway as he put his citation book away.

As they put on their helmets Bob said, "Why the hell did you stop, man? He would have never chased us tonight. He would have never caught us. We could have gotten away easily."

"The fence, Bob... Remember the fence?"

Bob shook his head and started his snowmobile.

The cop sat in the patrol car with the lights off, apparently waiting to see if Shawn and Bob kept their promise of heading back the way they came in. They waved as they passed the front of the car, creeping along at five miles an hour, up and over the hill, just the way they rode in.

After they were out of sight, Shawn took to the middle of the road and picked up speed. He didn't want to take the chance that the cop would beat them back to town and see them crossing in the middle of the village. He was afraid it would be too much of a temptation for the officer to resist writing a ticket in front of the town citizens.

They made it safely back to the barn and tucked the snowmobiles away for the night. Shawn and Bob thought they would keep this incident from their wives. There was no sense giving them ammunition if they didn't have to.

Several years later, as so often happens when someone tries to hide something, the incident surfaced at a neighborhood gathering. It was the summer just after Hawkins retired and moved onto their street.

Shawn and Amy and neighbors, Bob and Sandy, were sitting around having a beer when Bob asked their new neighbor, Mr. Hawkins, what he did for a living. When Hawkins said he used to be in law enforcement, Bob thought for a moment, staring at the man.

"You're not over in Mars, are you?" Bob questioned.

"Well, I used to be. Yeah, it was part of my territory. The whole township, yeah," said Hawkins.

"Do you remember two snowmobilers you stopped on a real snowy Saturday night, oh, years ago? Remember that? Was that you? The guy kinda looked like you, younger, though."

"Oh, yeah, yeah!" There was a pause, "I remember that, yeah, some night that was!" Hawkins said sipping his beer.

"Yeah, hey…Thanks again. Really glad you let us slide!" said Bob.

"I can't believe that was you," Shawn chimed in.

Amy and Sandy just looked at each other. Obviously, Shawn and Bob had some secrets they hadn't shared with their wives.

"Oh, okay, sure," said Hawkins. "Hey, you know why I remember you two so well? You know why that stuck in my memory to this very day?"

Shawn and Bob, grinning, shook their heads simultaneously.-

"Well, you two are the only *assholes* on snowmobiles that ever stopped for me. Really! Nobody on a snowmobile was ever stupid enough to stop for a cop that can't go more than five miles an hour." He howled and slapped his right leg.

Bob and Shawn looked at each other and stopped smiling for an instant.

Then Shawn said, "Well, we just wanted to do the right thing, ya know?"

Hawkins laughed louder, "No, I thought you two ran outta' gas there. I never thought you just stopped to give me a chance to write a ticket. We all had a good laugh back at the station later. Wow, never seen anyone so stupid. Funny. Just crazy stupid."

Shawn, a little upset and wanting to upstage this guy, said, "Nice. You know, we thought, before you let us go, you were going to screw us good. You know, maybe you were on a power trip. You sure seemed like it, small town cop with a big badge and a big gun and all. Real loud, pushy... and stuff."

It got very quiet and Shawn watched as Hawkins stopped smiling and turned red. He hastily added, "But you weren't. Well, I guess you weren't.... were ya?"

Amy said, "Shawn!"

They all looked at one another and started laughing again.

Shawn thought maybe he shouldn't have used that particular comeback; it may have made Hawkins feel belittled in front of his new neighbors. Ever since that time he had been civil but not really friendly to Shawn and Amy. He was a lot friendlier with Bob and Sandy.

"Yeah, I'd say he could still be angry," Shawn said. "Seemed okay today, though."

Amy had a habit of drinking a lot of water throughout the day. She believed it helped her maintain her weight and considered it much healthier than her friends' habit of smoking to stay thin. Shawn was into drinking water, as well, but usually liked it in the form of a brewed product; either with hops and barley or coffee beans. Shawn was adamant about not drinking anything alcoholic when he was driving, though, especially when he was snowmobiling.

Shawn preferred to have several cups of coffee early and then nothing until lunch. He found this worked well for him when he was traveling. Amy, on the other hand, who constantly sipped from a large bottle of water, did not. Consequently, on all but the shortest of trips, frequent "pit stops" were needed. Shawn wished they had some type of motor home with a bathroom so he wouldn't constantly need to interrupt the trip.

Amy would like to have a motor home, too. She thought it would be great to have a bedroom and kitchen handy at any time. Shawn felt she didn't get how much quicker the trips could be with fewer "potty stops" along the way. She had made so many stops over the years they have traveled together that Shawn suggested she compile a book of all the various restrooms she had visited. Amy shrugged off his remarks saying he'd be the one hurting from bladder or kidney problems because of his prolonged periods of not drinking enough water.

During the last potty stop, about 280 miles from home, Shawn re-inspected the towing set-up while Amy used the convenience store restroom. The only benefit that Shawn could think of with the stops that Amy required was that it gave him an opportunity to check the equipment.

Before he filled their extra gas cans, Shawn noticed the XMZ had moved; one of the hold down clamps had worked loose. Shawn grabbed his gloves from under the Jeep's seat and scrambled up onto the trailer to fix it. He didn't want to wait for Amy's help so he unclipped the cover on the rear of the large XMZ and took a firm grip on the bumper. The sled weighed over 600 pounds and had a carbide studded track which rested firmly on the wood surface of the trailer. It was going to take all of Shawn's strength to lift and slide the machine back into the right position.

With a sudden jerk, Shawn lifted and tried to slide the sled back to the right. Just as the slack in the suspension came off the trailer floor, something abruptly halted the upward motion. In his haste to fix everything, Shawn had forgotten to unhook the redundant safety strap Walt had connected.

Shawn heard a loud pop and felt a sharp pain shoot through his back and down his legs all the way to his feet.

He cried out and dropped the sled back onto the trailer bed and fell to his knees. Slowly, Shawn reached out and took hold of the sled's bumper. He stood cautiously upright, taking shallow breaths of the cold air. He hoped the pain would ease as he realized the trip he had longed for could be over just like that.

Gingerly, he stretched his back. It hurt the worst when he bent over and took a deep breath. Maybe, if he rode carefully, it would be okay. Shawn should have known better as it required a lot of upper body strength to steer a large snowmobile, especially at low speeds.

He was right about one thing: if Amy found out he injured his back, the trip would be over. Shawn's plan quickly became to hide the pain and not let Amy know about it. Otherwise it would mean heading back home and lying around the house for a couple days. He loved these trips too much for that, especially now that he'd be riding a dream machine!

He left the sled where it was, clamped the hold down and slowly replaced the cover.

As he inched over to the edge of the trailer, he glanced around the parking lot. He noticed a Hum-Vee that pulled up to the gas pumps in front of the station. Shawn thought briefly of the thousands of Army Hum-Vees he had seen in Iraq. While there were many civilian models around, it was strange to see a full military version alone on the streets in the states.

It appeared to have camo paint and non-issue, heavy black window tint. He wondered how a civilian got it. It even had machine gun brackets and empty rocket launchers. Maybe it was a back-up from a local military installation, although he couldn't see if the driver was wearing fatigues.

The thing just sat there; no one got out, no one pumped fuel. It was apparently waiting for something to happen or someone to arrive.

He noticed Amy leaving the front of the store. She was walking toward the Jeep. He had put it off as long as he could. It was time to climb down from the trailer.

He sank to his knees at the edge of the trailer's deck and then stepped down onto the parking lot. He shuffled to the driver's door and, grasping the door handle, turned and slid his butt into the driver's seat. He wiggled painfully until he was behind the steering wheel. He took some shallow breaths as he waited. Seconds later, Amy hopped into the Jeep and slammed the door. It rocked the vehicle and even that motion made Shawn moan under his breath.

Amy gave Shawn a long look.

"You okay, bub?"

Shawn moaned a little louder, intentionally this time, and said, "Ahh, ooh, can we get on with the trip now?"

Amy, looking a little puzzled said, "Yeah, sure, go." She added, "New cover?"

"New cover?"

"The one that's on your sled, *that* new cover. I didn't notice it before."

"Um,oh yeah, *that* new cover. Yeah, kind of a special. Had to buy some other stuff to get it," he muttered.

"How much?"

"You don't even want to know, Amy."

"Guess not then. I don't care. Who cares? Not me! Nope! It's only money we don't have. Why care?"

Shawn sought to change the subject.

"Hey, talking about how much stuff costs. Who did the clean-up on the computer? I checked the history and it's already been cleaned up, I mean really swept clean. You don't know how to do that, do you, Amy?"

"Oh, ah, ah, I had a problem with it and, ah, I had to take it in to have it fixed. Well, I was gonna take it in. But this guy at work knows a lot about computers and he offered to come to the house and fix it; some weird geeky guy at work. Yeah, he took care of it. He's good—weird—but really good."

"He must really know his shit. It was a better job than I could ever do. What did it cost?"

There was no reply from Amy.

"Amy, I said, what did it cost?"

"Oh, um, I don't remember, Shawn, a few bucks, I guess? Twenty, maybe, Why?"

"Wow, pretty cheap! He must've been there for hours. Pretty cheap for three or four hours. You sure that's it? That's all?"

"What are you getting at, Shawn? You're acting like I'm lying or something. Making things up. I told you I think it was twenty bucks. So, what? I'm lying about a lousy twenty bucks or something?"

"No, I'm not saying anything about lying, I just asked, 'cause he did such a good job. Seems like it would've been a lot more, that's all. Take it easy, Amy. Don't be so defensive... Jeez."

They traveled down the highway. Amy stared out the window and munched on caramel popcorn she bought at the store and sipped more water. Shawn drove silently and gritted his teeth at every expansion strip and pothole they hit.

THE TRAILHEAD

"Wow!" Amy yelled and bounded from the Jeep just as Shawn pulled into a parking spot. "Hey, look at the pine trees up here! They look like someone dipped them in marshmallow sauce and stuck them back in the ground. Wow, look over there!" She pointed to a hillside of evergreens and mountain laurel. "And there," she added as she looked at the smooth running stream. "Check out that cliff, Shawn," pointing to a large out-cropping of gray granite that had multi-colored icicles running clear to the ground. "F-a-n-t-a-s-t-i-c!" she proclaimed, grinning widely.

"What a place, Amy. I think we've died and gone to snowmobile heaven. Good idea coming up here…This is just *awesome.*"

Although they were only yards apart, they were shouting in their excitement; everything was covered with a recent six-inch blanket of fluffy, sound absorbing snow. There were no echoes. *It is surreal*, Shawn thought.

"This is like trying to talk underwater. Everything feels closed in, like I'm in a big stereo speaker. Neat!"

With his back feeling better, Shawn made a suggestion.

"Hey, let's unload and eat out on the trail. I'm sure we'll find a great place to take a break. Boy, if it's this good here, what's it going to be like up in the high country? Look,

Amy, this must be two feet deep along the edge of the trail," he stepped into deep snow not five feet from the Jeep door.

The area was void of other humans and there were only two other vehicles, trailers attached, in the corner of the large trailhead lot. This was one of the benefits to riding on a weekday. They knew this lot would be packed with snowmobiles and other equipment on a weekend. Shawn and Amy had it pretty much to themselves.

They were going to get to ride powder; also known as "breaking trail." The lead rider would forge into the virgin snow, usually the person on the biggest sled. A powerful engine was needed because they had to overcome the resistance of dense, untouched snow. The heavier sled would pack it down so others could follow. It took skill and stamina, but the ride was so smooth. Once multiple sleds had traveled on the trail it would develop moguls that either jarred you to death or that you took at speed and hoped you wouldn't be thrown off the trail. Powder was what true riders sought. The only thing even close was to be the first ones on a trail that has just been groomed as smooth as a highway. It was a treasured part of the snowmobiling experience.

Shawn cinched his kidney belt extra tight and began the unloading. Amy walked behind Shawn's sled and stopped suddenly.

She focused on the rear portion of the XMZ and said, "Better start talking…And *fast*, bucco!"

"Oh, um, ahhh… It's not what you think, hun."

"Oh, yeah? It's *exactly* what I think. And don't 'hun,' me! It's a new sled, isn't it? How *could* you, Shawn? We never even talked about this. We *always* talk about big stuff like this. Is this the new Shawn? Now that you're home don't

43

I have any say in how we spend our money? What's this about? Start talking... Talk!"

"I'm telling ya, it's not what you think!"

"What is it then? It looks like a duck, it walks like a duck...What? *What?*" She persisted, "It's not a damn duck?"

"It's just a favor from Jay Shamal. He felt bad for me not being able to get a new sled so he said I could use it. Just for this trip. You know, 'Break her in fer me, Buddy.' No strings, no obligations. Just a friendly gesture. Really, Amy, I didn't buy it. I'd never do that to you, to *us*! You know I wouldn't. You know me better than that. Right? *Right?*"

She stared at him for a few moments as she calmed down, then said, "You had better not be b.s.ing me or it's curtains, fella. Oh, I don't know Shawn... What if you break it? Something goes wrong?"

"Jay said not to worry about it. He's glad I'm back and everything's okay. He's just a real good guy. A real friend, Amy. I mean, it was strange...He really insisted! I was almost afraid to say no!"

"You had better take it easy, Shawn. 'Cause bet he'd want to be paid if anything happened. Mark my word, I know him."

"I will. You know I will." A very relieved Shawn gave her a quick hug.

"Don't touch me," she said with a laugh. "Let's get a look at this monster. Wow, it's awesome! Too bad you're not keeping it. Sorry. But you can't keep it, Shawn."

The rest of the unloading went without a hitch. Shawn remembered to turn the fuel cut-off back on but then struggled a bit to get the new sled started. While the engines warmed, Shawn and Amy donned their snowmobile attire.

Amy had long since abandoned the dark, 'turtle green' clothing from when she first started riding and now wore only bright colors. She figured reds and blues were more 'upbeat' and if she ever got lost, she would be easier to find. As for Shawn, well, he could have served as a fashion statement for his brand of snowmobile. When he bought his sled some years before, he went for the entire ensemble of clothing to match his ride. He was wrapped from head to toe in blue, yellow and silver gore-tex. The theme of the manufacturer at that time was cross country racing or "X racing."

Consequently, on almost every surface, including the rear portion of his helmet, there was a bright yellow X. He even joked about being the "X poster-boy" model for the sled-maker and, with his dark complexion, square cut jaw, dark curly hair and green eyes, he was good looking enough to be just that.

Although his suit looked great and was a fashion statement, at some of the back country bars and taverns they often found themselves, he felt a little conspicuous. They were frequently surrounded by people wearing the all-black coveralls or even ubiquitous Carhartts of years ago. He sensed others staring at him but had never had anyone say anything. Now, though, he was a mismatch to the XMZ colors of black, red and gold.

They mounted the sleds. They were ready and eager to go.

Snowmobiling has a tendency to make time seem to move quickly. It's important to concentrate on the task at hand: looking far ahead to avoid obstacles, spotting and committing to memory outstanding landmarks and taking mental notes of any signage and cross trails so that it is possible to get back to where you started. Shawn had found if you did your mental homework on the way out, you could rest your brain a little on the return trip and ride with less stress and more confidence, enjoyment and, above all, speed.

Shawn approached leading a group of snowmobilers much as he did most things in his life; with a lot of seriousness. It took away some of the fun but he had that kind of personality and this trait had been exacerbated in Iraq. He credited that with the fact that he had survived. Amy, on the other hand, tended to think more about the time the trip would take and where the important stops were along the way; scenery and "necessities."

The snow became deeper as the two penetrated farther into the forest. Snowmobiles can, in the right conditions, successfully traverse three to four feet of powder. A lot depends upon the amount of moisture and consistency of the crystals. The drier the snow, the greater the need for speed. On water, if one stops, one sinks. On snow at least, the results are not as catastrophic, but if one doesn't consider the snow pack it can lead to hours of digging a stuck vehicle free. Amy and Shawn knew how to avoid that; keep the sled moving and stop only after looping back over the top of your tracks, packing down the soft snow.

Snowmobile helmets fit tightly on the head. Ear plugs, which Shawn and Amy wore, combined with the helmets drastically muted external sound. However, the sound of your own breathing was loud and a sneeze or a cough could be startling. It is a strange kind of solitude and can become hypnotic. Even with the distant hum of the engine and the necessity for tracking the condition of the trail, it is easy to become mesmerized and lapse into a 'zone.' The rider begins to feel as one with his machine which is the goal of pristine snow and a perfectly running sled. It actually feels a little like flying.

Amy began to daydream and was thinking back to the time she and Shawn visited Canada near the little town of Minden. It was just after a snow storm, late in the season, and the snow was about three feet deep. Each morning they traveled across a large, frozen lake about two miles wide and fifteen miles long. Theirs were the only tracks to be seen. They followed tree limbs used as trail markers, poking up through the deep powder, carefully placed by dedicated, local club members.

When traversing the smooth lakes, Amy and Shawn found they could let go of the handlebars and steer by leaning their bodies right and left, much the same as a motorcycle is ridden. By simply tilting their heads and shoulders to one side or the other, they could make long, sweeping changes. It was a magnificent discovery for Amy. Shawn, a physics teacher, already understood weight distribution, center of gravity, and other aspects of polar movements but for Amy, this was an empirical discovery. She remained fascinated by it.

And so she would, from time to time, attempt to replicate that method of steering. Today when she tried it, it worked and she rode this way for quite a while; leaning left, leaning right—rounding out the slight curves in the wide trail. She snapped back to reality, though, when one of her skis caught in a rut and sent her careening towards a ditch! Being the experienced sledder that she was, the scare only lasted a split second and she grabbed the handlebars and corrected the direction of the sled. She was glad she was riding behind Shawn because he hadn't seen her antics. Amy knew if he saw her doing something that could get them in trouble he would really give her a hard time. She wanted Shawn to believe she needed a slower speed so he didn't go uncomfortably fast.

On they went, threading their way through the tight tree-lined corridors, crossing meadows and plunging back into shrouded passages. Shawn was thrilled to be back on a sled, especially a sled of this caliber. He was enjoying the terrain, appreciating the machine, and clearing his mind of the bad things he had experienced in recent years. Getting to do this with his best friend was what it was all about, and he cherished it.

Amy and Shawn were making good time averaging between 30 and 40 mph. The conditions were perfect for frequent bursts of speed that would take them as fast as 65, sometimes even faster. Most of the trailheads were marked with speed limits of 45 but the posted speeds were much lower where there were sharp turns and dangerous conditions. Out in the open though, experienced riders would up their speed considerably. There was always the major risk of getting a speeding ticket because of radar used by local and state police, however.

Shawn was stunned by the level of performance of the XMZ. He still couldn't believe he got to ride this amazing machine! Jay was quite the guy.

About an hour into the ride, they started a long ascent on a very steep logging road. The switchbacks were numerous and very sharp at the crease of the mountain sides, slowing their progress considerably. After reaching a higher altitude they were quickly shrouded in a misty cloud layer that slowed them even more.

After ten minutes of straining to see the trail through the opaque white wall, Shawn had enough and pulled off to the right side of the narrowing trail and stopped. He watched, motionless, as the mist streamed rapidly up past them. He assumed they must be near another switchback but couldn't see more than a couple of feet through the fog.

They sat patiently on their sleds waiting for the funneling effect to clear out the mist. It took another ten minutes.

When the last wisps of clouds dissipated they couldn't believe their eyes. They had stopped about twenty feet from the edge of a drop off. They climbed carefully off their sleds and simply shook their heads. Shawn thought about the barbed wire fence he and his neighbor almost rode into. That would have been really bad—but this would have been fatal.

They stood quietly, each in their own way giving thanks they had stopped when they did. Finally, Amy muttered, "Wow…Close!"

Shawn didn't say anything.

The roadway was solid so they decided since they were already stopped they might as well break out the sandwiches and hot soup Amy had packed. As the air cleared the view became spectacular. They had reached about 2,000 feet and could see a lake on the valley floor in the distance; the scenery was breathtaking!

"Hey, how's that crotch rocket?" asked Amy as she unpacked the food.

"Super! Can't believe the power. I'm not even pushing it and it's so much faster than mine. They've come a long way since I've been gone."

A bald eagle swooped over them and down through the valley below.

Shawn said, "Wow, neat! Think how an eagle feels when it's flying in these mountains. It gets to see this kind of terrain all the time."

"Yes, but when an eagle is flying it's all about survival; no prey, no life!"

Shawn nodded in agreement. He valued survival, too, now more than ever.

Amy's comment reminded Shawn of the time they were shocked to see a blue jay swoop down and knock their cat, Tiger, into their pool. They and their neighbors were left speechless as the bird flew off into the woods, screeching loudly all the way. Shawn wondered if the attack was for fun or intuitive. It wouldn't have been for food; the cat weighed about 15 pounds. It only happened once but had made the cat wary for several weeks afterward.

They sat side by side on Shawn's sled, drinking in the magnificent view as they ate their lunch. They talked about the chances of seeing any other riders on a weekday and agreed that it would be rather slim.

It made them both think of some previous rides they had with Amy's aunt and uncle and some of their friends. All of them would have been on this ride if Aunt Betty hadn't passed and Uncle Bud hadn't taken retirement seriously and moved to Florida's Gold Coast.

Shawn and Amy had some fantastic times with them and their friends, Bill and Jan. Bill told some stories that had Shawn laughing so hard he cried.

One recollection led to the next. This time it was the trip to Northern Michigan—their first all day ride in that region. Early on in the ride, Bill, who was a loud, boisterous, gentle giant of 6'4" and nearly 300 pounds, was riding in the lead. He loved to use his large, heavy machine to break trail for the others. He was following the trail, keeping it slow and safe and being careful not to deviate more than a couple of feet from either side of center until about ten miles out. They rode out of the wooded trail and onto a 200 foot wide, cleared power line area. Bill uncharacteristically decided to leave the trail—and leave the trail he did!

Plowing through two feet of soft snow he would look over at the rest of them and grin so big it could be seen through his face shield. Then he would wave and punch the throttle—his big sled throwing a rooster tail high in the air. He would slow, wait for the others to catch up and do it again. The third time, he looked over, grinned and nodded. He clamped the throttle wide open but this time, the skis dipped into a four foot drainage trough running across the width of the clearing.

Sno-mo Bill, as they affectionately called him, didn't have time to stop grinning as he flew over the handle bars. He found himself planted face first in the snow covered field. Luckily, his sled tipped at a 60 degree angle and was undamaged. Bill, on the other hand, was convinced he was mortally wounded.

Bill was kneeling in the snow pawing wildly at his face shield and screaming. At first they thought he had suffered some kind of seizure, but once they got closer they realized what was going on and could hear, "I'm blind! I'm blind! I'm blind! Oh no! Oh, God, no! I'm blind!"

As he turned toward his companions, they could see what had happened. They all began to laugh, sinking slowly into the snow.

Bill eventually settled down as some of the snow fell out of his helmet and he could see daylight once again. All

Bill knew was that his eyes were open and he couldn't see anything but white. It took a good half hour before they stopped laughing to themselves. Bill claimed later that he just pretended to be scared. His friends never bought it, however.

There were many other stories, each better than the last and fun to recall.

Shawn and Amy laughed out loud as they finished their lunch. They both became silent as they remembered their funny foul-weather friend, Sno-Mo Bill, wasn't with them anymore. He had died several years before from a massive heart attack. His wife, Jan, and their friends, Butch and Karen, had all quit riding. Uncle Bud and Aunt Betty retired and then Aunt Betty passed away. Shawn and Amy were the only ones of the group who still rode.

Remembering those past rides and the loved ones they shared them with was sobering and momentarily dampened the exhilaration of their current ride. Shawn had recently had to endure the loss of a number of close friends in Iraq. He was now more hesitant to make friends as he thought about the fleetingness of life—and the suddenness of death.

INVITATION TO DINNER

A low growl intruded into the solitude. It slowly built to a roar. In a minute or so, four snowmobiles came out of the woods toward Shawn and Amy.

About the only way riders can greet one another when meeting on the trail is by a nod or a wave. Amy and Shawn did just that as the four riders roared by.

Snowmobilers are a friendly species, as a rule, and snowmobile etiquette deems it proper to see if help is needed if a sled is stopped on the trail. It was pretty obvious that Shawn and Amy had taken some time to enjoy the view and grab a quick bite of lunch. However, after stopping fifty feet or so past Shawn and Amy, the group's leader climbed off his sled and carefully made his way back to Shawn.

He lifted his face shield. "Pretty up here, huh?" he asked, looking closely at Shawn's mount. "Nice sled...Yeah, *real* nice."

"Sure is. Thanks...It's a rental. Hey, how far is it to the lake down there?"

"15 or 20 miles by sled. I guess it'd be about seven or eight as the crow flies, probably. Never seen a rental like that before. You guy's been up here before?"

Shawn replied, "No, but wish we had. It's just beautiful. And the trails are excellent. Who takes care of them?"

"Well, not the state, that's for damn sure." said the man. "We do. I'm Big Jim Markus from the High Markers

Snowmobile Club," he stretched out his large gloved hand for Shawn to shake.

Squeezing, with enough force to pain Shawn's hand, he laughed adding, "Markus-High Markus...High Markers...Get it? That's our clubhouse down there to the left of those white pines. Just above the front tip of the lake. See it?" he pointed with his other hand. "It's pretty big really. Looks kinda small from here, I guess."

"Oh yeah, yeah," Shawn replied as he squinted, searching for the clubhouse and not wanting to admit it was too small for him to locate.

Shawn broke the handshake and said, "I'm Shawn Kaan. My wife, Amy," he looked over to where she stood. He added, "Hey, thanks for the great job on the trails. Is there a trail fund? I didn't see a collector can at the trail head parking lot. I'll pitch in if you have one."

As soon as he said it, Shawn realized he would probably need to open his wallet, currently stuffed with vacation cash and fork over some of it to a complete stranger; four of them, in fact, in the middle of nowhere.

"Nah," barked Markus. "We expect it from returnees and the regulars but not first timers. That's why I asked before. No, we get together in the summer and do the clearing. The state kicks in on the price of the groomer and operator. You guys are welcome to enjoy it. If you want to stop in at the clubhouse for a drink and some venison, go ahead. We've got the wives down there cookin'. Drag-races are tomorrow. You can kick in for that and help our trail fundraising that way. Where'd ya say you rented that monster?"

Shawn looked at Amy. She shook her head and packed up the lunch leftovers. He realized they needed to get back to the parking lot and get going. They still had a long drive.

Shawn said, "No thanks. We're headed up north tonight. We're going to ride around the Black Caves wilderness area. But thanks for the invite…Oh, I didn't… I rented this from a friend, a good friend."

Markus seemed unable to take his eyes off the XMZ and responded, "Yeah, some friend. I'll say. That's a damn good friend. You really should stop awhile. You've probably never seen a game feast like ours." He added, "The Caves, huh? Just the two of you goin' up there?"

"Yup," Shawn said. "Couldn't find anyone else to come along. Most of our friends are working this week. What, rough up there?"

"Well, it's pretty wild. First timers should have a guide. I'd go as your guide if we didn't have this drag race and game feast thing all weekend. It'll be the middle of the week before we get back to normal around here. It draws about a thousand people. I usually get the leftover stuff to do. But it's worth it, for the club I mean…Pulls in enough for new trail equipment every year or two."

He stopped as he thought over his schedule and added, "I guess I could head up, though, later in the weekend. But you'd be all done ridin' by then. It's tempting, though, sure is nice up there. Well, we'll see."

He then added, "Oh, what the hell! Come on down for a bite. Meet the members and we'll talk more about it at the clubhouse. Come on, I'll lead. It's only a couple a miles. You'll like it, guaranteed, or there's no charge. We're lookin' for new members anyway." He laughed and looked back at his riding companions. They all nodded agreement.

Shawn looked at Amy again and, surprisingly this time, she shrugged her shoulders as if she was letting Shawn make the decision.

She said to Markus, "I've always wanted to know what wild game tastes like. Shawn used to try to hunt a few years ago and...well...I never got to try anything 'cause he never wanted to shoot anything."

"Oh, you a softy?" slapping Shawn on the shoulder. "You'll love this then, Sweety. A little bit of everything!" said Markus. "Okay, then," he shouted to the other three riders, "Let's kick some snow back on up where it came from!"

He walked briskly back to his sled and mounted it.

"Stick with us!" He yelled back.

Amy looked at Shawn and said, "You think we really need a guide up there or is he just shootin' the bull?"

Just then, before Shawn could answer, the sleds roared to life and within seconds the group was back into the tree line and only the diminishing sounds of their engines could be heard.

Shawn simply shrugged his shoulders and shouted, "Come on, Amy...We'll lose 'em!"

They took one last look at the beautiful view and climbed quickly onto on their sleds.

Amy shouted to Shawn as she strapped on her helmet, "Bud and Aunt Betty would've loved this, huh?"

Shawn replied, "All of 'em would've loved this!"

Amy nodded her head, flipped down her helmet's shield and turned the key. Her engine snarled to life and she jammed the throttle wide open. Her front skis lifted off the snow and she was into the wood line ahead of Shawn. He was surprised at her abrupt takeoff and he followed, shaking his head.

They penetrated deeper into the forest, catching a periodic glimpse of drifting snow crystals from Markus and the others. The group finally slowed, allowing Shawn and Amy to catch up.

Shawn and Amy were really enjoying this ride. Even though they were going faster than their usual speed, it was relaxing since Shawn wasn't breaking trail. Amy enjoyed the challenge of keeping up with the boys and knew Shawn couldn't complain about how fast she was traveling in order to do it. In fact, Shawn had his hands full just keeping the four friendly strangers in sight. Shawn knew his sled could easily handle the speed; he just didn't want to wreck it.

The scenery was spectacular and the trails circuitous. The off trail short-cuts were among the most beautiful they had ever seen. It was obvious their new friends had been around this mountain a lot, picking and choosing the perfect balance between speed and lean to maneuver easily between the mountain laurel and dark pines. Bursts of seventy miles per hour were not uncommon on the open flat stretches. Down they went, sometimes approaching descents as steep as 45 degrees or more, with the throttle on as they ran the sides of the mountain. At one part of what turned out to be the fourteen-mile ride, they climbed up and down a double, smaller mountain peak that hadn't been visible from the higher elevations. One at a time, they tackled a 60 degree, eighth of a mile climb, stopping at the narrow summit for a few seconds to catch their breath, and then plunging down the other side. Ride at Your Own Risk signs were posted frequently indicating the wide-open pathways were the courtesy of a gas pipeline company that stored natural gas reserves deep inside the mountain.

Amy and Shawn had never before put themselves to a test like this. The power of the sleds was exhilarating, especially Jay's XMZ. No, actually it was intoxicating. The XMZ's hundred and eighty horsepower was hard to hold onto at times, especially when the carbide studs in the track bit deep into the firm hard-pack. Even Amy's sled, with only half the power of Shawn's ride, launched her much lighter weight skyward at times. It was a euphoric, intoxicating and addictive experience, not unlike what pilots experienced when accelerating hard. Shawn had felt it before when he was transported by the 82nd airborne choppers. The hot landings and take-off's squeezed his breath out as he hunched in his seat during rapid acceleration; the blood leaving his head so rapidly that he would get light-headed. He liked the sensation. It would remain a good part of his military experience, and now part of his snowmobiling, as well.

It was only a thirty minute ride but seemed longer because of many sights and challenging thrills. One at a time, they crossed a frozen stream on a long, swinging bridge made of wood. They had to slowly pick their way through a trough where they were surrounded by head high boulders. Shawn could only wonder what was in store for them at Black Caves since Markus regarded it so highly compared to this area.

They glided out of a patch of dense pines into a meadow and the clubhouse came into view. It was very large with a wrap-around porch. It was made of huge white pine logs and had a modern garage tucked in behind it.

Everything was green, white or natural wood colors. The garage door was wide open with a couple dozen snowmobiles scattered within, hoods tilted up and people working over the engines. Shawn looked back over his shoulder at the mountain face and wondered how he could have missed this large a compound.

He squinted as Markus came up beside him, "Yeah, see the overlook where we first saw ya?" he pointed up and way to the left of where Shawn thought it to be.

Shawn said, "Sure, right there, near that opening." He pointed very close to where Markus did.

Markus, Amy, and the others started to laugh and Markus said, "Nah, sport, I was just pullin' yer chain, it's over there," he pointed back in the direction Shawn had originally thought it was.

Shawn, a little embarrassed, said, "Well, great, then. I *was* right. I was starting to worry I'd never find my way back out of this valley."

Markus said, "No, let me tell you, it's easier to get out of here than where you're headed. We took the scenic route comin' in. If you'd get lost leaving here you'd make a right turn just past our swingin' bridge and follow that old loggin' road up to the overlook, then keep goin' to the parking lot. Gotta watch that road past the overlook, though, 'cause they still plow some of it when it gets blown in. Tough on the skags, too. Lots a gravel. Go on in!" he pointed toward the front door.

Shawn and Amy stepped up onto the porch and Shawn opened the door for Amy. He took a step back and said, "Go ahead in, hun...I've *gotta* check out the race sleds, just for a second."

Amy, with a surprised look said, "Oh, all right, but don't be too long; I don't know anyone here."

The smell of roasting meat filled the air. The tables sported red and white tablecloths with small brown, antlered deer heads in a pattern repeated every six inches. On these were pots, pans, tin trays and plastic storage containers. The large, log-walled dining room/meeting area was surrounded by dozens of real stuffed animals. The ones that drew Amy's attention were a coyote, a wolf and a cute little bear cub that was sitting on a log in the corner. A short, smiling, middle-aged woman carrying plates and napkins saw Amy studying the displays.

She said, "Oh, that cub...so cute, huh? No one shot it. It was hit on the road a couple years ago. The State Game Warden figured we could use it. So one of the guys stuffed it. We didn't eat it or nuthin'. I've eaten bear and they're pretty tough," she added.

Amy wondered if there were any of these left in the area when the woman added, "There's probably a thousand others out in the forest right now. Too bad they don't know enough to stay off the highway. The wolf's the rare one. Big Jim Markus got him up near the Provincial Park near Black Caves. Ya know Big Jim?"

"Uh, oh...yes, we just met him," Amy said, "He must be some hunter."

"You betch'a!" the woman responded. "And good guy, too. He did *all* this," she pointed around the room.

Amy said, "Wow, that's a lot of food."

"No, dear, not the food; we brought that. The place, I mean the place, the clubhouse. He built the clubhouse," the woman said and nodded positively.

Amy could just manage another "wow" as she meandered beside the huge floor to ceiling stone fireplace. It made her think of pictures she had seen of old Adirondack mansions.

"This must have taken a long time."

"Pretty much a whole lifetime," said the woman. "He started as a kid. Always wanted to own a camp. Well, this'd be a camp if I ever saw one," she laughed. "Big Jim does a lot for the local's. A lot of folks are just barely gettin' by around here. So he'll bring in some money, *somehow,* from the outside and spread it around to those of us that can't do much on our own... Guess you'd be one of those from the outside?" she laughed.

Amy said, "Yep. Down across the Pennsylvania state line. We're just up for some snowmobiling today. We're going on further north tonight. It's real nice around here, though. Riding is just beautiful! Hey, can I help do something? Anything? I've just been talking and gawking and not doing anything to help."

The woman reached across the table from where Amy was standing and offered her hand.

"By the way, I'm Connie. And, nah, we're almost done. People are gonna start comin' in soon. Guess we coulda' picked a better day to have this dinner. We're supposed to get some real heavy, windy stuff later tonight and no one seems to know how much to expect up here. Don't know about you guys but I'm fixin' on stayin' the night if it gets bad out. I'm not into playin' in the snow like the rest of you."

Amy responded with a hardy shake and said, "I'm Amy Kaan. Nice to meet you. My husband Shawn is outside looking at sleds."

Connie said, "Oh, yes, those boys and their toys. Can't seem to ever get a snowmobile they're happy with. They're always gettin' em in and fixin' em up and getting' another in and fixin' it up. Buy, sell, buy, sell and on and on. Must'a had fifty come through in the last month or so. Me, like I said, not much for snow. Probably be better off livin' in the south. But then again, this is like our own country up here. We pretty much do whatever we want. Closest real town is a good twenty-five miles away. Guess I'd miss that. Something to drink, honey?"

"Oh, uh, just water. Thanks," Amy replied as she picked up a glass from the table.

Probably ten people had carried bowls, eating utensils and drinking glasses to the table when a man opened the wide plank door. The wind gusted and blew it open all the way catching the man off guard. It hit the wall with a loud bang and some light snow scattered across the pine floor. Some of the place settings at the table needed attention as the wind re-distributed napkins and placemats; some onto the floor.

"Good thing the dishes are heavy," Amy said quietly as she looked toward the man struggling to close the door against the cold blast. She realized it was Shawn with an armful of cordwood. He was barely able to carry the firewood, let alone control the door. Amy quickly dashed to his aide, closing the door and giving him a curious glance.

"Whew! It's kickin' up fast out there." Shawn said loudly between huffs of breath. "Thanks, Amy."

He didn't notice all the work he had just undone. Shawn strained to carry the logs close to the fireplace as Amy steadied the load with one hand.

He said, "Thanks. Hey, nice place, huh Amy?"

"Sure is. Do you know that Markus guy built this?"

Shawn responded with some surprise, "Yer kiddin'. Wow! Well, he almost needs a wheel chair to get around in here after what I just saw."

"What? What happened to him?" Amy asked.

"He was standing next to a race sled that was running. Up on one of those stands like I wanted to get?" Shawn replied as Amy looked blank.

"You know, it lifts the rear end of the sled so you can run the track and not move the sled forward. You know, to set the track up... adjust tension and stuff. Like I wanted to buy before I left?"

Amy quickly grew impatient with his unnecessary details. She still didn't know what he was talking about.

So to get on with it she replied, "Oh, sure, I remember. So what'd he do? What happened?"

"Well, it fell off the stand... the race sled. It came down on Markus' feet. Lucky he had good boots on 'cause the sled had studs. And the guy had it pretty well cranked up just before it came off the stand."

Amy's eyes got big and she heard Connie, now close behind her, gasp a little.

Connie responded, "Is he okay? Did they call the doctor?"

"Nah," said Shawn. "It really didn't do too much. The guy must've let off the throttle just before it dropped down and the track hit in the front first. It was pretty much stopped when the back landed. I've never seen such neat little holes punched into boots like that, though. Must be steel toed like my military boots. Good stuff. He was really lucky."

Just then the door swung open and Big Jim Markus slid in on the snow dusted floor as if nothing had happened. Jim weighed in at two hundred fifty pounds and stood six feet five so he filled the doorway. He closed the door with a thud and carefully placed his helmet and coat on a rack behind the door.

Without hesitation he wrapped his arms around Amy and squeezed, "Did I hear I'm lucky? No, hubby here is the lucky one. You're cuter than I thought with your clothes, uh, helmet off," he laughed.

Amy was expecting something about the incident outside and was caught off guard. She stammered and tried to think of a good response but only said, "Well, looks like you're all better, big boy." Amy was uncomfortable with the familiarity the hug indicated.

"Ah, yeah, all better. Like my place?" Markus said as he looked around and slapped his sides.

"Beeeautiful!" Amy and Shawn said in unison.

"Good! Glad you like it. Twenty bucks upstairs if you're stayin' in a bunk for the night. Mine is in there," Markus said as he nodded to a door beside the fireplace and winked at Amy.

Amy, now even more uncomfortable and wondering what had gotten into this guy said, "Sure, bucco, and I guess that one's... *kinda'* free?" as she turned and walked toward Connie a table or two away.

Since Shawn hadn't seen the wink, he added with naiveté, "How could it be free, Amy. I mean if the others are twenty a night?"

Markus just grinned at him and shouted to everyone that had filtered into the large room, "You guys 'bout ready to eat? I know I'm starved."

The response was a unanimous "Yeah!" from kids and adults alike.

"Well, let's sit down then. Ain't gonna serve us standin' up, ya know," he added.

As Markus sat down at the middle of the first table he said, "Amy and Shawn. Over here...I have a place for you over here," pointing across the wide table from his seat.

Amy hesitated.

Shawn quickly said, "Great," and headed for the seats.

Amy followed more slowly and found she was seated directly across from their host who she believed was hitting on her. She was not happy. She thought Shawn had put her in a precarious position. Amy was a beautiful woman and didn't appreciate the guys that were regularly coming on to her. It has been tough with Shawn gone. There had been temptations and she was glad Shawn was home and they could be together. Markus' obvious interest was unwanted and, thankfully, he seemed to get the message.

The remainder of the late afternoon meal went well. Shawn and Amy sampled dishes they had only heard about. Amy noticed Markus watching her eat and felt a little uncomfortable but she had been there before and simply ignored it. One thing she knew for sure, they would *not* be staying the night!

All in all they had a great time. The conversation was loud and lively. There were a lot of jokes and genuine, old fashioned camaraderie with a small town feel. Shawn told Big Jim the story about Jay, his snowmobile dealer friend and the XMZ. Jim thought he had heard of Jay but had never met him and would certainly like to someday.

A Storm to Remember

The time passed quickly and twilight began to settle in over the valley. Latecomers to the event spread news about the impending storm. It seemed a strong nor'easter had unexpectedly developed off the east coast and was intensifying more rapidly than they first thought. Now, apparently, the National Weather Service for the northeastern states was calling for high winds, an additional foot of snow to the east, with possibly more on the mountain ridges. As a scientist Shawn knew nor'easters this time of year could be ferocious and unpredictable, especially in the mountains. Shawn was thinking even with all their satellite technology sometimes old Mother Nature still had a few surprises up her sleeve.

Shawn and Amy finished dessert, placed a twenty-dollar bill on the table in front of them and announced that they intended to leave before things got too bad. Someone said that the wind was already howling outside; they might want to re-think their decision and stay over.

They reaffirmed their intentions, thanked everyone and began to put on their suits. Markus, concerned, suggested they scrap their plans to ride back up the mountain and again urged that they stay the night.

"You know, 'cause of the bad weather, we'd forgo the twenty bucks here. I've seen it get real heavy up by the trailhead. You oughta' wait it out with us, being this was my idea and all, I'd feel bad if you guys got stuck or lost that new sled goin' back up there," he said with genuine concern. He cast a glance at Amy to see her reaction.

"Nah, we'll be alright," Amy said coolly as she opened the door letting in the howling wind. "But thanks for the offer. This was nice, really, thanks a lot!"

Shawn shook Markus' hand and said, "Hey, thanks a lot. Maybe we'll see ya again sometime, and, ah, nice place. And great food everybody! Bye," he shouted again as he waved and glanced quickly over the room.

"Got enough gas?" Markus barked. "Remember to turn at the top of the logging road," he added.

"Yeah, okay!" Shawn yelled through the howling wind as he stepped outside the door. "No problem!"

Markus spied something across the front yard of the compound and grabbed Shawn by the sleeve and pulled him back to the door. "Hold on a minute," Markus shouted. "George and Vicky are gettin' ready to pull out, too. You can follow them part of the way. Least up to where the first turn is. Shit! I haven't seen the wind this strong down here in long time," he shouted.

Shawn grabbed Amy's arm and shouted over the wind, "Go ahead and start the sleds. I'll be right over."

Amy nodded and Shawn trudged through the deepening snow to where George stood beside his smoothly running machine, the exhaust swirling furiously about the cowling.

Shawn yelled through his raised facemask as the man made a futile attempt to clear the blowing snow off his seat.

"Hi, I'm Shawn," he yelled. "Markus said to follow you guys up the hill. We're going to the trailhead," pointing almost skyward.

"Okay!" shouted George, a tough, good looking man in his late sixties. He pushed his face close to Shawn's, "But I'm not goin' slow! We'll sink in this powder if we go too slow. Can the other guy keep up?" he pointed toward Amy.

"Yeah, my wife!" shouted Shawn, "She'll be okay."

George just nodded. He climbed on his sled and pulled over toward Amy. He nodded to her and pointed in the direction they had come in.

Shawn walked to Amy as she sat, engine running, and yelled, "Hang on and follow them. We're gonna be *flying!*"

She nodded and then looked ahead, wriggling her gloved hands on the handlebars. She turned the heat to "max" on the grips, realizing she wouldn't have time to do it while they were moving.

Shawn mounted up and pulled alongside George. He looked at Amy and then Vicky. George opened the throttle on his older, smaller sled and shot away following one of a dozen trails through the brush and back into the woods.

For the first several miles their progress was brisk. But once they crossed the swinging bridge and hit the open logging road George picked it up considerably. The snow fell heavily and Shawn stayed back about a hundred feet or so just so he could see ahead. Between the heavy snowfall and the rooster tail from Amy's sled his view of the logging road was nearly obliterated.

Shawn didn't dare glance at his speedometer for fear of rear-ending Amy's sled if she stopped quickly. He

69

guessed they must be going in excess of 70 miles per hour. Shawn had only been riding the XMZ for a short while but had noticed a change in the sled's windshield at around 70. It had a tendency to lean back and dip in the center at that speed. It was doing that again now, but a glance at the passing scenery and the way the sled was handling didn't equate with the speed. Finally, looking quickly down, Shawn noted the speedometer was only showing 30 miles per hour. That had to mean the headwind must be around 40. It was a sobering moment for Shawn and he began to wonder if they had made a huge mistake. He felt certain that Amy wanted to leave and now they were in for the long haul.

At what looked like an intersecting trail, they caught up to George and Vicky who had pulled off to the right and waited. Shawn pulled up beside George. No words could be heard because of the helmets, heavy snow and howling winds. George pointed straight ahead and made a hooking sign indicating a right turn. He then held up six digits. Shawn assumed the turn was six miles away. He nodded his head and gave George a thumbs-up, and a pat on the back, acknowledging he understood and to say thanks. Amy, sitting on her sled, was starting to worry about the worsening conditions. The new snow was well over a foot deep now and coming down even heavier than before. They could hardly see fifty feet ahead. The skies were getting darker as the daylight rapidly disappeared.

Wiping snow from his face shield, Shawn looked back at Amy. She nodded. He waved his left hand and pulled out across the intersection, blowing huge amounts of powdery snow in his wake. His speed was considerably slower than George's; he didn't want to take a chance on wrecking the sled.

As the two traveled the ridge, they realized they could be in real trouble. Shawn's gut feeling was seldom wrong in Iraq and it was making itself felt now. Although he believed he could make it out of tight spots, he seemed to know when it was going to be close…and this was going to be very, *very* close.

The trail was fairly straight but drifted snow, piled three and four feet deep, made the road appear to have sharp switch-backs. Shawn crept along at about five miles per hour but the horizontal snow confused him. He felt like he was traveling much faster. He was on and off the throttle, abruptly climbing the drifts, snow and wind blowing over the hood and windshield, into and under his facemask. This was so disorienting that as he attempted a look at the odometer, he turned slightly left into a snow bank. The sled began to bog down in the deep mound. Shawn gave it full throttle and the sled responded, spinning the track and then gaining traction on the hard edge of roadway. He climbed quickly out of the trough and shot about five feet into the air, landing with a bone jarring thud.

Shawn, not used to so much power, didn't expect a leap like that and momentarily released the throttle. That was all it took and the heavy sled settled into a cradle in the snow. The hood was half buried and the seat was even with the snowy surface. Shawn had a sickening feeling and, as he got off, sank another foot. Amy had managed to stop on the trail. She slogged through the thigh high snow to Shawn, concern written all over her face.

"Son of a bitch!" yelled Shawn toward the sled. He leaned toward Amy, lifting his facemask to shout over the howling wind.

He yelled, "Now… Now we have a *real* problem."

71

Amy looked around at the trees, the branches so heavily laden with snow they were bending all the way to the ground. The wind was constant; howling and screaming through the trees, boughs lashing. Amy recalled a similar sound when a tornado damaged their house and took away part of their neighborhood a decade ago. She began to think of what they would need to survive the night on this ridge in the storm. She had heat packs, matches and candy bars in her sled's storage compartment but no blanket or shelter and no shovel. She began to feel foolish about being so upset about Markus' comments that she had let it put them here, in the middle of *this*.

Shawn tried to lift the sled out of the deep snow by himself but to no avail. Amy pulled on the skis while Shawn pushed and used the throttle. The sled dug in but only moved forward about a foot. Shawn had Amy pull from the side, afraid too much throttle would find six hundred pounds of snowmobile running over the top of her. After ten minutes they stopped; exhausted, panting and sweating. They had managed to move the sled only twenty feet uphill toward the snow filled logging road.

Shawn thought it might be better for Amy to ride the sled, working the throttle and shifting her weight from one side to the other, while he pulled on the skis. It worked and the sled popped out onto the trail. They shouted with relief and then collapsed on the seat of the sled, gasping and exhausted. After a couple of minutes they realized they had better get going. They still had a long way to go and there could be even worse problems ahead.

Shawn realized his right ring finger felt tight and would barely move. He pulled off his glove and tried to make a fist. All of his fingers but the one responded. He couldn't feel it and figured he must have dislocated it when he was trying to jerk the sled from the snow. He yanked it straight out. With a loud pop and a sharp pain he could feel through his entire right side, the finger began to move again. He wondered how it was his back didn't bother him, but figured it would probably show up later. He mused that adrenaline was a marvelous natural anesthetic.

Amy was impatiently waiting. She signaled for him to get going and Shawn nodded, put on his glove and resumed their interrupted slog through the heavy snow. As they fought through the deep drifts the sky seemed to lighten a bit and Shawn was able to make out the sides of the trail.

The cleared trail they had started their ride on was all but obliterated by the deeply piled snow that had accumulated on both sides of the roadway, leaving only a deep V shape to ride in. There was only a narrow area just wide enough for the snowmobiles skis.

Shawn kept the sleds moving at about ten miles an hour and tried to look back over his shoulder from time to time to check on Amy's where-abouts.

Several miles later, Shawn saw a huge cloud of drifting snow blowing across the logging road ahead. He was approaching it slowly and glanced back at Amy to make sure she was okay. Amy was frantically waving her arm. Shawn quickly turned forward and slammed on the brakes.

Chills ran up and down his spine.

"Oh shit," he said to himself. "Oh shit!" He stood on the running boards, staring at the trail ahead. "Oh, man." Talking to himself out loud, "Oh man. Wow."

There, fifty feet ahead, pulling into a turnaround on the right side of the road was the biggest, fourteen-wheeled snow plow he had ever seen. It was huge! The lights were on but the snow it displaced completely hid the truck from Shawn and Amy's view.

Shawn realized if he hadn't gotten stuck, they would have been in the deep trough—no escape, blinded by the blizzard—with a fast moving, fourteen-wheeled monster coming at them head on. The driver would never have seen them and there was no way they could have ever gotten out of the trough and out of the way. They were very lucky to be alive and deeply grateful for the divine intervention.

The huge truck sat idling. Shawn wasn't sure if the driver even saw their sleds. He was afraid it could still turn or back into them. With a quick snap of the throttles, they passed the turn-in and moved on to the much smoother, faster surface of the newly plowed logging road. They picked up speed and Shawn's windshield never budged, indicating the wind gusts were now drastically reduced. The worst was over.

Several miles running on the smooth logging road brought them to the parking lot at the trailhead, just like Markus had said. The huge plow had pushed a lot of the heavy snow out of their way.

They pulled up directly behind the trailer and climbed stiffly off the sleds, leaving them running. Shawn's back had begun to tighten up and was hurting him now that the ride was over. He had a tough time stooping down and adjusting the ramp to load the sleds, but with Amy's help—after first using the outhouse—they were soon ready to load up and get rolling.

After the sleds were loaded onto the trailer, they sipped some lukewarm tea in the Jeep as the engine warmed up. The heater felt good as their chills slowly abated

74

and the realization of their close call with the blizzard and the road plow dissipated.

They held each other in a tight embrace and said how much they loved each other. They laughed when Amy softly sang a verse from the Simon and Garfunkle song, "...Still crazy after all these years, oh, still crazy after all these years."

Shawn said that he had had time to think and worry during this ordeal; an opportunity he never found during dangerous moments in Iraq. As he put the Jeep into drive, he added, "Ya know, a lot of people think riding snowmobiles is a cake-walk. Well, I'm thankfully still here to say, it isn't!"

They pulled slowly onto the road north again and Amy repeated her comments about the evergreens, now looking more than ever as if someone had melted marshmallows and poured it all over them. Their dark green boughs stood in stark contrast to the snow.

"What a place, even with that storm." Shawn said, "Wow. I think since we made it through all that, this trip is really gonna be worth it. We'll have tons to talk about."

Amy responded, "Just pick it up a bit. All that hard riding and this tea, I'll need to stop again pretty soon, you know."

Shawn *did* know and uttered a mild groan as they hit the first of several deep potholes on this stretch of road.

They later learned they had experienced the worst storm to hit that area of upstate New York in more than fifty years. Amy cried when she heard on the news that several people who had been at the game dinner never made it home. They were eventually found, frozen to death where they had gone off the side of the swinging bridge.

A ROUGH PASSAGE

They had to drive through deep snow for several miles. The plows hadn't cleared the road they were on and it was quite a while before conditions began to improve. Their old Jeep had no trouble pulling the trailer with the snowmobiles, however, and they finally were able to maintain a steady 40 to 45 miles per hour.

"Hey, Amy, who's Brad?" Shawn asked.

"What?" Amy was startled.

"I was just wondering who Brad was."

"Well, where'd ya come up with that one?"

"You know, I heard you call me that this morning."

"And I *told* you I didn't... I *didn't* call you that. I'd have no reason to call you that. I said babe, it was *babe.* Get it? And get those ears fixed like I said, Shawn. That's Shawn. Notice, I called you *Shawn*, Shawn?"

"Is that the guy that fixed the computer, Amy?"

"No, NO! Well, so what if it was. Well, I don't know, Shawn. Nobody at work really knows him too well. He's new, maybe... What are you getting at? Who cares?"

"I care! If you call me by some other guy's name in the morning. I care."

"Oh," she moaned. "And I care that *you* care, Shawn. I said babe. That's final, Shawn. Unless you're calling me a liar and a cheat it's end of story. And if you *are* you can just

76

turn this thing around 'cause I'm not interested in doing *this* all week."

"I never said the word 'cheat,' all I'm asking is who this guy Brad is."

"Okay! *Okay!* He's the computer nerd. Happy? And I said his name out loud, so what? I see him every day, Shawn. It was an honest mistake. No big deal. It wasn't like I was having an orgasm when I said it, I was sleepy. Maybe I was thinking about the computer. I don't know. Okay? You done? Is this interrogation over, Shawn? Or *not?*"

"I guess so. I just didn't expect it, another name. You know."

"Shawn? Quit!"

Fifteen minutes passed and there was no conversation. Amy put in some of her new CD's.

"That's new stuff," quipped Shawn. "When did you start listening to that crap?"

"Oh, well, see, my stud bought it for me, Shawn, of course. You're too much, Shawn."

She popped the CD out of the player and plugged in her MP3, adjusting her earpiece and looking straight ahead with an angry look on her face. A heavy silence filled the vehicle for a long time.

Just after crossing into Canada, they passed a big wooden sign proclaiming "Welcome to Canada" along the right side of the road. They were picking up momentum on a long downhill curve when, unexpectedly, they saw what looked like the scene of an accident. There were four dark blue and yellow New York State police cars and two black Royal Canadian Mounted Police 4x4's blocking the road.

The lights on the tops of the vehicles were flashing. There wasn't a lot of room between the Jeep and where the cars had set up the roadblock. It caught Shawn off-guard.

He eased on the brakes and quickly realized that wasn't going to work. He panicked and hit the brakes too hard. The Jeep pitched forward and the tires squealed as they fought for traction on the gritty, salted tarmac. Shawn quickly regained control but not before six or seven police officers darted toward the safety of their cruisers. Shawn could see their startled looks all too clearly, even with the darkening skies.

"Oh, shit." Shawn yelled out loud." What the hell *is* this? Are they *tryin'* to get killed or what? Assholes!" he added as he slowed to about twenty miles per hour and felt the effects of a huge shot of adrenaline prickle across his skin.

Shawn suspected his unexpected arrival could cost him a ticket, at least.

He slowly approached the group that had re-assembled at the blockade, one or two with hands resting on their holstered weapons.

Just before Shawn stopped the Jeep, Amy mumbled something about being right about the gun that Shawn tried to bring.

She looked at Shawn and said, "You didn't sneak that damn thing in here, did you? You *did* leave it at home, Shawn. Shawn?" she almost whispered.

By then, Shawn had the window down and was ready to speak to the officer, an older Canadian Mounty that stood at least six foot and two hundred and forty pounds. Before he could say anything, the Mounty spoke.

"Well, I'm sorry, sir. Guess we could've picked a better spot for our picnic, eh?" smiling wryly.

Shawn began to smile back, when the Mounty added, "Would you turn off the ignition and step out of the car please. And you, too, Ma'am," he said seriously to Amy.

Amy immediately climbed from the Jeep. Her legs felt shaky and she was still not sure if Shawn had taken the pistol out of his duffle bag. They could be in real trouble here.

Almost immediately another Mounty and a New York State Trooper began to walk slowly around the Jeep, scraping the windows to look inside. Another one, using a flashlight bent down on one knee in the slushy roadway to look under their SUV and trailer.

One of the Mounties stepped up onto the trailer and partially uncovered the sleds to look at the registration stickers and vehicle identification numbers located on the side of the running boards. He held a paper in one hand comparing the numbers on each sled.

Shawn tried to explain he was caught off guard but was cut off by another Mounty. The officer said, "That was some pretty stupid driving there, fella." He added, "Let's have your license, registration and insurance card, eh?"

Shawn handed over the paperwork. He managed to add, "Sorry, you guys are kinda' close to the bend. I never expected a road block out here. I thought... I thought it was an accident."

The Mounty took the cards, turned and walked toward the other officers. He stopped, turned and walked slowly back to Shawn.

"You're from the U.S.? Passport's also, please," with an outstretched hand.

Amy leaned back into the Jeep, hurriedly searched through the debris covering the back seat and handed him a sealed plastic sandwich bag that contained their passports.

As the Mounty again turned away, he said out loud, "He thought he was gonna get to hit a wrecked car instead of you guys, eh?"

While everyone laughed at the comment, Shawn knew the officers were not amused by his driving style. The New York State Troopers talked with the Mounties a few minutes and then several approached the Jeep where Shawn and Amy stood.

The Mounty handed the cards back to Shawn and said, "You guys are from where? Below New York State? Uh, Pennsylvania? Where are you headed?"

Amy called up one of her 'look how cute I am' smiles and stepped in front of Shawn, closer to the officer.

"Up to Black Caves to ride for a couple days, sir. Look, I'm sorry about my husband's poor driving. I have to go really, *really* bad and told him to drive faster than he should've. Sorry for the scare." She added quickly, "Are we in trouble here or getting arrested? 'Cause if we're not, like I said, I gotta go *really* bad."

Shawn cast a wide-eyed stare at Amy and couldn't believe that she was trying this on an angry cop that they had almost run over.

Shawn then added, "Yeah, she's got a kidney problem. Ah, from drinking too much water on trips. It's, um, pretty bad."

After he said it, he knew it sounded really pathetic. The Mounty just stared at Shawn for a few seconds then turned back to Amy and smiled.

"No, everything seems to be in order, Hun. You can go. Just travel a little slower. Okay, Sweetie?" he said with a wink.

As they turned away, he added, "Oh, ah, you don't have anything to declare, do you? Weapons, produce, contraband?" Shawn and Amy instantly shook their heads and turned and climbed quickly into the Jeep.

"Oh, you're missing a sticker on the one sled, ya know," said the one New York State Trooper as he leaned in the opened window, probably checking for the smell of alcohol.

"Ah, it's a borrowed sled from a dealer and I thought everything was on it that was required," Shawn protested.

"It's not a permit or anything. You're missing a *Trail Watch* sticker on the big sled. You want one for it? Here ya go," handing Shawn an envelope. "We do appreciate the help."

Shawn, relieved, took the material and said, "Oh, sure. Ah, yeah, I'm… well, I *was* a military guy. Always willing to help out law enforcement."

"The trooper smiled and said, "Yeah, I'm aware of that. Thanks again."

Shawn no sooner got the window up when Amy said, "That jerk! The Mounty. What a womanizer. Just looking at him I knew he'd be easy."

Even she was surprised her scheme worked so well.

81

"'Okay, Sweetie' he said," she continued. "Ha, Sweetie!"

Several officers watched as they were waved through. Shawn pulled slowly past and onto the open roadway. He wanted Amy to keep her comments to herself, afraid one of the officers would hear her.

He picked up a little speed and passed some cars waiting on the southbound side of the road. He mused on how Amy could use her charm on the Mounty and then make fun of the guy for falling for it. Shawn thought to himself, it must be a woman thing; drawing in the prey and then deriding him for going along with the program. He thought of times when she had probably used similar tactics on him, then figured it would be too depressing to add them all up. One thing was for sure; she had charm and knew how to use it.

They gradually increased their speed until they were running at about 30 miles per hour.

Shawn said, "I know what you're thinking and, no, I left it at home, like you said. The gun, it's at home. Guess I'll admit to that one being the right choice. That could have been the whole enchilada right there. Whew! Very close, Amy. And since there's no one around to hear me, I'll say it aloud, you were *absolutely* right... *dear.*"

Amy was still smiling at her accomplishment in getting them off the hook and said, "Good! I wonder what *that* was all about? There must be something up. And what's with this missing sticker thing?"

Shawn said, "Oh, they're just watching all the borders closer now 'cause of the bad guys that slipped into the U.S. You know, those terrorists out in Washington State. Or maybe the ones from Buffalo, or the ones getting in through Maine. Maybe even drug stuff, who knows, could be all of that since 9/11."

He continued, "Oh yeah, the stickers. Shamal put some on your sled. Guess he forgot the XMZ. It's a new Homeland Security program the New York State Snowmobile Club started: *Trail Watch*. The members are supposed to help identify suspicious people or events while out riding the trails. You know, help out the Department of Homeland Security and stop the bad guys."

"Sorry, *I'm* not stopping any terrorists, Shawn. Nope...not doin' it."

"You don't really stop them, Amy. You just report them. *They'll* stop them."

"Okay. That's better then. I can do *that.*"

Shawn was trying to put all his identification cards back in his wallet while he drove. Amy hated it when he did this, taking his eyes and attention from the task at hand. He unconsciously slowed as they rounded a bend. A car rapidly caught up with them and then, as if surprised, backed away just as quickly. Shawn handed the wallet to Amy.

"Here ya go, can't get them back in there. Besides, I'm driving here."

"No kidding...I wish you wouldn't do that."

"Yeah...okay. So nice up this way, I can't believe you'd have to worry... "

He stopped talking while he gazed into the rearview mirror. He recognized that the outline and headlights behind them belonged to a military Hum-Vee. He was quiet as he wondered how the guy had passed through the roadblock so fast. He wondered if this was the same Hum-Vee from the gas station. He was puzzled as to how a U.S. military vehicle could just drive across an International border like that. There could be civilian Hum-Vee's around these parts, but it seemed unlikely.

Amy, not noticing Shawn's quiet, abruptly broke the silence and said, "I wish it was like it used to be years ago. We never even thought of that kind of stuff happening. Ya' know, all the terrorism crap. It's so bad now, I'm not sure I want to bring kids into this kind of world. It just keeps getting crazier and crazier. 'Course we don't know for sure if that's what it was or not, but it sure makes ya' think about it, huh?"

Shawn nodded his agreement and thought that might not be something he would like in his life right now; the added worry of kids.

He added, "But our kids would be smart, huh? They could dodge bullets all day long, having parents like us. They could do that, huh?"

Amy forced a smile and said softly, "Um, I guess so."

She looked toward the windshield and closed her eyes wondering if they had reached that point. Shawn watched the rear view mirror as the Hum-Vee lagged farther and farther behind.

UNSCHEDULED STOPS

One thing Shawn overlooked when he had tried to shift the XMZ and hurt his back was the fuel level in the Jeep. Had he not been trying to keep Amy from finding out he was hurting, he might have thought to fill the extra gas cans, as well. With a relatively small tank, the Jeep was normally good for around three hundred miles, but towing snowmobiles, trailer, and supplies, the gas mileage dropped significantly.

As they traveled farther north, signs of civilization diminished. Hills had turned to mountains, it was dark and the snow began to fall again. The wet roads had turned to slush. Even more worrisome to Shawn was the orange light on the instrument panel that began to flicker the gas pump icon, indicating there were only a couple of gallons of gasoline in the tank. Shawn resisted telling Amy the bad news.

Before he could say anything the orange light steadied and sounded a low chiming. Amy knew what that meant and snapped her head toward Shawn. He asked her to check the map for the next town that looked as though it might have a gas station. Yawning and without the expected comment, she reached into the glove box and withdrew the Northeastern United States/Canadian map. She turned on the overhead light and studied the map quietly for about a minute.

From what she could tell, the next town appeared to be about thirty more miles north. It must be small as the population and amenities did not appear on the map, just the name of the town; Lands End, Number 4. It seemed a strange name but they were aware old lumber and mining towns often kept their original names and Shawn and Amy didn't think much of it. Amy reached up and turned off her light and they quietly traveled on.

The little gas pump image on the dash was even brighter now, lighting Shawn's face with a soft orange glow. At least the warning bell stopped, he mused. He wished he could shut the light off as well so it didn't wind up being an issue for Amy, but he couldn't.

Shawn had waited as long as he dared and now reluctantly slowed the Jeep and pulled the shift lever on the floor into the 4-wheel "lock" position. The road conditions were worsening. He had refrained from using the four-wheel drive as long as possible because it decreased fuel mileage drastically. He had figured thirty miles was well within the reserve range but that was in two wheel drive. He doubted they would make it to Lands End.

They had both noticed there were very few vehicles on the road and those they met were covered with heavy snow. The tension mounted as the darkness was now absolute. Their windshield wipers were struggling with accumulating snow and ice and they had not seen a sign of another car going in their direction for the past hour.

Shawn and Amy rode quietly, exchanging few words. Suddenly, the headlights lit up a large warning sign DO NOT PICK UP HITCHHICKERS. They mutely looked at each other and thought back to a trip they had taken through Arizona years ago. They were out in the middle of the desert north of Phoenix and saw several Do Not Pick Up HITCHHIKERS signs.

Their faces grim, they looked at one another in disbelief, realizing what this meant. Lands End #4 was not a town at all, it was a Provincial Prison. Just then, the engine started to sputter.

Here they were, out of gas at the worst possible place, under the worst possible conditions, with drivers instructed not to pick anyone up. Amy was livid.

"You asshole, Shawn!" she shouted. "You absolute dimwit! How could you be so damned stupid? You, the greatest of all 'safety-nicks' and worry warts, I can't believe this. If we get out of this alive, I'm going to kill you. Trust me. It's a done deal," flipping her hands in the air. "I...I...I can't believe this," she muttered and started to bite her nails as she turned toward her window.

Shawn didn't reply as he rolled the Jeep to a stop, just yards from what appeared to be a dark, unused entrance to the prison. As the power steering ceased to respond, the lights shone on an old grey sign with a large # 4 in the center. He couldn't read anything else but he knew where they were. He had difficulty getting the rear of the trailer off the road and turned on the emergency flashers. When he tried to restart the engine, it immediately fired. He heaved a sigh of relief and quickly put the Jeep into gear. As it gained power and began to move smoothly back onto the roadway, he looked smugly over at Amy.

"And what was that? Lose control for a minute, did ya? Huh? I'll take that apology now, I..." his voice trailed off along with the engine, and once again he rolled the Jeep to a stop, this time just past the dark entrance.

"Up yours, Braineack. What? Did you think you just mysteriously found enough gas to get us to somewhere safe? Guess again, toots, we're screwed. I can't believe this. I just can't."

Shawn told her about his back and blamed that, and the price, for not filling the tank. He was hoping for a little sympathy but it was not forthcoming; only a directive.

"Get your butt outside, soldier and start suckin' on a fuel line on one of the sleds. With any luck, you'll swallow some and I'll collect the insurance. I can't believe you did this to me, Shawn. Think about it...you're supposed to be a smart guy. How smart is this? Moron!"

Shawn had enough and gave in to the stress of the moment.

"Well," Shawn retorted, "I don't know about you, smart-ass, but I'd sure feel a hell of a lot better if I had the gun I wanted to bring with me...*with* me. What about *that*, Moron?"

They sat quietly a moment and then Shawn fumbled under his seat. He yanked on his work gloves, grabbed the flashlight, and stepped into the dark and the blowing snow. Amy stayed in the Jeep.

On his way back to the trailer, Shawn figured even though the XMZ used more gas, it also had a larger tank. Chances were, even after their ride earlier today, it would have enough gas left to get them to a town ahead.

He took off the gloves he had just put on and removed the cumbersome clips and straps from the front half of the snowmobile. Balancing on the balls of his feet on the narrow upright edge of the trailer, he tilted the hood open to gain access to the carburetors, fuel tank, and fuel lines. The wind kicked up and slammed the hood back onto his bare hand-scraping the side of his face as it past. He grabbed the handle bars to keep himself from falling, swore and reopened the hood. This time it stayed open. He lit the engine bay with the flashlight and noticed a gloved hand holding the hood open. It was Amy, bundled up and ready to help but with a glare at Shawn that matched the sub-freezing temperature. Nonetheless, her help was welcome and Shawn set about cutting the fuel line on Jay's new sled in order to siphon gas from the tank.

As he worked, Shawn thought back to when he was fourteen. He had a neighbor, slightly older and prone to trouble. This guy liked to take his sister's Renault Dauphine for joyrides and he wanted his buddies to go with him. In retrospect, Shawn knew they were stealing the car, but as teens they simply rationalized it as borrowing. Shawn's contribution to this wayward juvenile adventure was to siphon some gas the night before from any nearby vehicles so they would have enough for a nice, illegal ride early the next morning while their families slept in. Because of the number of times he had done this, Shawn became proficient in the art of siphoning gasoline, rarely spilling a drop.

As he forced air in and out of the line to get the siphoning started, he had a fleeting memory of the time they were caught with the car by local police. They were all under the legal driving age except Shawn's older brother who was behind the wheel. He had a learners permit and actually paid the greatest price. At that time, not getting your regular license until eighteen was possibly the worst punishment a teenager could be dealt. Of course, being grounded for the rest of the summer didn't go over well with the others involved, either. That episode forever ended their joy riding, Shawn now knew, for the better.

Shawn's distraction caused him to miss the critical instant to remove his mouth from the end of the gas line. He swallowed some gasoline and fuel started pouring from the plastic hose as Shawn gagged and retched. Amy grabbed the hose and filled one of the gas cans. Finishing what Shawn had started, she managed to get most of it in the Jeep's tank.

Back in the Jeep, with the heater on high and the strong smell of gasoline enveloping them, Shawn opened his door and heaved the wild game dinner and gasoline he had swallowed. He thought that perhaps Amy would feel bad about him vomiting several times, but to no avail. All the while he heaved, she scolded. *Relentless,* Shawn thought. *Well, maybe the bruise on his hand and the scrape on his face will bring a respite.*

He did feel pretty foolish for forgetting to top off the fuel, though. He couldn't really argue that point. After a mouthful of snow and the use of one of Amy's alcohol wipes, Shawn was ready to drive again, although he still felt pretty sick from the incident.

Just two miles down the road, after rounding a long curve, they saw a dimly lit, very old gas station just visible through the blowing snow. A sign beside the narrow road read, 'Welcome to Lands End pop. 53.' Amy and Shawn thought to themselves, *No one lives here but prisoners. No wonder it doesn't show on the map as a town.*

Shawn pulled into the station. The storm was worsening by the minute and there were no other cars to be seen. Bundling up, they quickly filled the gas cans, snowmobiles and the Jeep. They wanted to take no chances from here on out.

The old station was dirty but Amy once again needed to use the facilities. They walked into the office to settle the bill and locate the restroom.

When they entered through the squeaky glass door they spotted the attendant. He was perched behind a dark brown wooden counter, its top piled high with greasy shop manuals and service bulletins. It was all haphazard; in some places spilling onto the dirty floor. The curved glass front of the cabinet had some large cracks and a couple of holes in it. Displayed inside were gas and radiator caps scattered randomly on the dirty shelves. The floor had a black layer of hardened grease that stuck to Shawn's boots as he walked. The place smelled like burnt motor oil.

The attendant was at least seventy-five. Shawn thought he looked like he had weathered a lot of tough winters. His hair was off-white and unkempt and he was wearing old wire rimmed glasses and a heavily soiled gray sweater over a dark blue shirt, the collar buttoned closed. Hunched over, he scowled at Shawn as he scratched at a week old growth of white stubble. As Shawn approached, the old man picked up a crusty pair of binoculars and peered at the gas pump.

Amy said, "Restroom, please?"

The attendant continued to peer through the binoculars as he said, "Behind me. Door's open, eh?"

Amy said, "Oh good. Thanks."

"One fifty two, eh?" This was muttered with a strong French-Canadian accent.

With a surprised look on his face, Shawn reached for his wallet.

"Whoa! One fifty two? Oh, I forgot! Oh, yeah, I need the amount in American... I'm paying with U.S. dollars," Shawn spoke loudly and with deliberation.

"Oh, well then, let's see, eh?" the old man said, counting on his fingers. "U.S, eh? Well, ah, that'll be O-n-e h-u-n-d-r-e-d f-i-f-t-y t-w-o, eh?" slower, louder and more deliberately than Shawn. He sat there and glared as if daring Shawn to question his pronouncement.

"Really?" Shawn questioned.

Shawn slowly began to count out the money.

"Boy, I thought we had an edge on the currency thing up here. Guess not."

"Well, sure ya do, sonny, eh? Look here, I'm sellin' 'ya the big Imperial gallons a gas up here. An yer payin' by the litre. An gettin more of em, I might add. Jus' look at the numbers on my pump there an you'll see, eh? You have one fifty two, at whatever per... Why, you're gettin' more'n your share of the currency thing up here. Yup, you 'mericans make out like crazy on us poor Canadians up here. You have a nice ride now, eh?" ending the conversation.

Shawn said, "Yeah, okay." He turned toward the door, still slightly puzzled about what just transpired. He figured the old coot just charged him over $5.00 a gallon.

Amy will figure it out if she ever comes out of the restroom, Shawn thought. Then he began to think maybe he should use the restroom, too, just in case it turned out to be a long time before getting to their destination. He turned back toward the old man to ask about using another restroom. When he did, he saw the old guy at the open end of the counter adjusting a picture frame on the wall behind him. Then, apparently unaware Shawn was still standing there, he turned and rolled down his right pant leg. Shawn could see that he was covering the barrel of a sawed-off shotgun strapped to his leg.

Shawn felt his third surge of adrenaline of the day and facing the old man, managed to say, "Ya got another one?"

The old guy looked a little flustered as he finished adjusting his clothing.

"What, a cut down 12 gauge?" he snapped.

"Uh, no, restroom," Shawn said looking at the old guys leg.

"Nope, broke," he spit out."Don't be a wuss, eh? Go 'round the corner an' piss like a man! Go ahead. Round that corner over there. Do it in the drain," he flicked his index finger as if directing a dog to the dark bay of the station. "I do. Won't hurt ya none, no one lookin' 'round here. Eh?"

Shawn nodded and moved to the dark area indicated. Relieving himself, not really sure where he was aiming, he shouted back over his shoulder, "How come you have a shotgun hidden on your leg?" He couldn't believe he had said it out loud.

"Cause I wanna, eh?" The low reply came from the dim doorway just behind Shawn.

Shawn was not comfortable with his back turned to this strange old man with a gun, and he sure as hell didn't want to brandish his 'wares.' He slowly turned away from the doorway and the old man. He wasn't at all sure he had done the right thing here... *and where was Amy, anyway?* Shawn wondered if they had stumbled into a bad situation. He figured he could take down this old codger if need be, but he was worried about the 12 gauge at such a close range.

Amy bounded into the doorway, surprising them both. She stood right behind the old attendant.

"Okay...Done!"

Shawn was relieved when he realized she was okay. He left the darkened bay and the old man slipped behind the counter.

"Bout twenty years ago a couple 'yanks' came in here shootin' up the place, eh? See here?" he pointed to the cracked glass in the case and several holes in the wall and door behind the counter. "Came up to get their drug buddy outta jail. Lucky fer me I was cleanin' my side arm at the time. We had a gun battle right here...fer, oh, 'bout five whole minutes. It was sumpin', eh? Shot me in the throat. Couldn't talk good fer years. N' killed my dog. Picture over there," he pointed next to his register. "But I killed one a them bastards, too, eh? I was so pissed. Other one got away. Never did find him, I guess."

Amy and Shawn stood there, mouths open, too shocked to say anything.

"So that's why I got it. I'm closin' up now," he suddenly sounded tired as if re-living the ordeal had worn him out. "Have a good un, eh?"

He snapped off a bank of light switches and turned toward Shawn, saying, "Ridin' up in Black Caves? Be careful with the cutie here, she's sumpin'," he winked and nodded toward Amy.

Shawn said, "Oh, yeah, I will, and thanks. Good luck." Not wanting to miss his first opportunity he added, "See ya when we come back, eh?"

The old man mumbled something like 'yanks' under his breath and Shawn and Amy ran laughing to the Jeep.

They climbed in, wishing they had left the Jeep running and the heater on. Shawn said, "Weird, huh? Guy's really lucky he had a gun."

Amy ignored the dig and simply said, "What a clean restroom! You'd never guess it from the outside. Needs some holes patched up...but *really* nice."

Shawn, flashing back to his fraternity parties, thought he knew why the old guy directed him to the dark bay to relieve himself while Amy was in the restroom... and why he called Amy a cutie. How did he know what she was like under all the coats and scarves? Shawn mused to himself, maybe the old guy needed that to get through his day; grab a chance and take a peek. It was pure speculation on his part so he decided not to mention it to Amy.

As they eased back onto the road, Shawn still thought he had been had by the old-timer. He was also frustrated that he couldn't convert liters to gallons quickly anymore. He sought Amy's help in a roundabout manner.

He said, "Okay, here's a hypothetical, Amy. If you had a wholesale business and bought 152 liters of perfume, assuming 4.5 liters per *imperial gallon*, but 3.78 liters per U.S. gallon, how much would it cost at $1.09/litre?"

Amy looked over at Shawn and said, "You can't help but let yourself get screwed, can ya? Let it go, Shawn. We're on vacation. Anyway, the old guy deserved a tip. You heard what he said about me! At least he wasn't a womanizer like that damn cop was."

Shawn just smiled then belched more gasoline fumes.

LATE ARRIVAL

They rolled into Lac Dranna, the small lakeside village they would call home base and from where they would ride over the next several days. Although it was now almost 10:00 PM, it was surprisingly busy. The trip had taken much longer than they expected; the feast, road block and gas incident adding length to an already lengthy day. Shawn had planned the trip and he was pretty accurate when it came to mileage; however, his estimate regarding time was way off. They both looked at their watches and wondered at where the time had gone.

Shawn realized he had underestimated yet again and thought back to the time they had taken their boat on the Erie Canal in Upstate New York. Shawn calculated the trip would take five to six hours. It took closer to ten and he almost had a mutiny on his hands. The boat had an open bow without a head or port-a-john. The pictures of the trip, taken in progression, revealed the loss of support for "Captain Shawn" as bright, cheery faces turned glum and impatient toward the end of the ordeal. Shawn had tried to speed things up, so much so that he was reprimanded for going too fast by an unexpectedly beautiful female lockmaster on the outskirts of Rochester. Shawn had a little bit of an alibi then, since the lecture at the last of the eleven locks took quite a bit of time. In reality, though, Shawn miscalculated a branch canal they had traversed some three hours away.

Shawn took solace in the fact that to appreciate a trip such as that, one needed to relax and savor the moment—like fine wine—slowly and with deliberation. Amy, along with the other couple, thought otherwise; especially when there was only one rest stop the entire trip. It happened that it was a dumpy old marina, very similar to the grungy gas station Shawn and Amy stopped at in Lands End. It had old gray wooden boats stacked all over the place. In retrospect, Shawn wondered about that proprietor as well. Had he, too, checked Amy out when she used the rest room? He had also directed Shawn outside for relief. Shawn began to think voyeurism wasn't as uncommon as he once thought.

As they approached the center of the small town, Shawn and Amy saw two men circling each other. There were about twenty people around them and it looked like a serious fight was underway. They pulled up across the street to watch and within a few seconds the men pushed, shoved and swung their way close to the Jeep. The rowdy crowd followed the action and quickly surrounded the men, and the vehicle. It scared Amy as the crowd taunted and cheered the fighters. The larger man pummeled the other and slammed his head into the Jeep's hood.

Shawn had his window up and it was a good thing he did because the smaller man had his head mashed against Shawn's window. His face was bloody and battered. He looked straight into Shawn's eyes. Then he glanced at Amy, obviously desperate. Shawn thought the eyes seemed familiar. He looked to be Middle Eastern.

Amy yelled at Shawn, "Help him! Help him! Do something, Shawn!"

Shawn reached for the door handle but the weight of the two men kept it from opening.

Surrounded by the angry mob, Shawn couldn't get out of the Jeep if he wanted to; and he really didn't want to. He had seen some pretty bloody fights at his school and in Iraq. He knew how quickly you could get hurt when you tried to separate fighters, but he had an idea that might work.

He grabbed the cell phone and acted like he was calling the police. Both men were tired and the fighting slowed and finally ended with a shove. However, the look in the eyes of the bigger man was enough to send chills up and down Shawn's back.

The victor stared through the bloodied glass at Shawn with disdain. It was almost as if he was saying "you're next." Maybe he blamed Shawn for ending the fight too soon. A wild and almost joyful rage was all over the large man's face as he battered his enemy; now that look of hate was directed at Shawn.

Shawn never liked backing down, but in this case, with the crowd outside and Amy in the Jeep, he would have to ignore his ego and try to get them out of this without injuries. He put the Jeep in gear and began to move forward—slowly at first, and then faster. He watched in the mirror as the victim slumped to the ground. The large man stood back then reached out and slammed his fist against the salt guard on the front of the trailer, all the while staring at Shawn. It was several minutes before Shawn could say anything. They pulled over near a gas station a couple of blocks away from the incident. An ambulance went by in the opposite direction just as they stopped.

"Damn," Shawn whispered, his hands and legs shaking a bit.

Amy, too, was speechless. Finally, she said solemnly, "Wow, what a welcome that was! Ya think that guy's gonna be okay? He looked pretty bad, didn't he, Shawn?"

Shawn said, "I guess so. Probably go to the hospital. Did you see how that big guy stared at me? Crap, Amy, I thought I was gonna to be next! Where the hell are the cops up here when you need them? Oh, I know, sitting down the road scaring the tourists. Damn, I think that guy was really pissed at me for picking up the cell phone. What an asshole. You know, when people like that get that look on their face, I think they could kill somebody. That wacko ought to be sent away for awhile. Must've been something serious or he would never have smashed the guy's face like that! Wow, very nasty."

They sat in the Jeep for several minutes before Amy said, "I have to take a whiz, Shawn. Be right back."

"Where are you...?" Shawn asked, trailing off as he realized they were in front of yet another gas station; one of Amy's favorite stops.

As he waited, Shawn began to feel the ache in his back again. He had probably been sitting too long and the intensity of the fight and the resulting melee hadn't helped. He sighed and then noticed a small, self operated car wash along the left side of the gas station. He decided to pull the Jeep in and clean the blood from the window. Shawn wanted to forget about the whole thing.

He drove into the bay and put in the quarters and began to clean off the blood. There was a lot more of it on the door than he had imagined and he wondered if Amy wasn't right in her appraisal of the damage to the smaller man.

Amy found Shawn finishing up and climbed into the back seat. She opened the cooler and took out a bottle of water. She simply crawled over the front center console to reach her seat. Shawn replaced the hose on the wall rack and climbed into the driver's seat.

Amy said, "Good idea. Don't want that dried on there. Did he dent the hood?"

"Amy. How can you worry about that when the guy might be dead?" He paused and added," No, I looked." Hesitating again, he said, "Scratched the door with his front teeth though."

Amy said, "Oh Shawn, no. He didn't... Did he?"

They looked at each other as he shook his head and nervously chuckled about something they realized would never, normally, be considered amusing.

Shawn backed the Jeep out of the wash bay and then drove forward.

"I sure hope the rest of 'em are friendlier up here. Maybe they've all got the Wild West mentality or something. I've started to think that Markus guy was giving us a warning when he said to be careful up here. It's been screwed up since we left... except for the sled ride. Maybe we'll get enough great riding in to forget the bad stuff, huh?"

Amy said, "Oh, I think it'll be okay, Shawn. The people in the gas station were fine. They did say, however, that there has been a lot of fights and stuff lately because of immigrants taking over a lot of the businesses and jobs. By the way, we'll go about another five miles and look for the "Westside Inn" sign on the left. I'm gettin' really tired now. I'll bet you're half dead. You never got a break."

Shawn just managed, "Uh huh."

Shawn thought that perhaps he was right about the victim being Middle Eastern. He hoped they hadn't come into an area where outsiders and foreigners, especially Muslims, were being persecuted. Shawn, although not a Muslim, knew he looked to be of Middle Eastern descent. In Iraq, he had seen Islamic extremists attack westerners. It didn't matter if they were Christians or Americans. He had seen Americans attack Middle Easterners, too. It didn't make any difference what their religion, when someone is a racist there is only a 'me' and 'them' mentality.

The Cool Westside Inn

Shawn and Amy located the Westside Inn with no further incidents. While Amy went in to register, Shawn started to unpack the Jeep. Amy climbed the seven steps and entered the small lobby, beautifully trimmed in dark, hand carved hardwoods. There were Adirondack chairs arranged in different groupings to encourage cozy gathering places. Some were near windows overlooking the lake and some alongside reading lamps set on small tables with fresh bouquets of flowers. Worn but well cared for rugs were laid over dark, plank floors. A wide set of wooden steps wound to a landing at the second floor level.

An old woman appeared from behind the small doorway at the rear of the office and smiled at Amy. She said softly, "And you must be Ms. Amy Kaan?"

Amy said, "Yes… Hi. Sorry we're so late. We had a couple things slow us down. Is everything okay with our reservation? Did you get our deposit alright? I didn't get a confirmation but I talked to... maybe your husband? He said everything was okay last week."

The old innkeeper slowly turned the check-in book toward Amy for her to sign.

"Oh yes, it's fine. Sometimes we're booked weeks in advance but this year things have been a little slow. Not sure why… The dog sled racers aren't here 'til next week so it's no problem. You're here into the weekend? Come on, I'll show you to your room, dear. It's upstairs."

102

Amy said, "Okay. Shawn, my husband, is bringing our luggage."

Just then Shawn entered the lobby. He was heavily laden with both arms full: two duffle bags, a small suitcase, and plastic shrouded shirts on hangers. He had obviously attempted to bring everything in one trip.

"Oh, Shawn," Amy said, "You're gonna wrinkle all those shirts!"

The innkeeper stopped on the first landing, turned and added with a chuckle, "If he was mine, he'd be iron'n those in the mornin', eh? Got one here ya know, an iron."

Shawn said, "Oh, they'll straighten out. Permanent press, right?"

The woman said, "Well, we're pretty easy goin' up here. No one's gonna complain about some wrinkles in your clothes." She chuckled.

They turned right at the top of the stairs and walked to the end of a long hallway. They passed five rooms, all with their doors standing wide open.

"We'll be riding most of the time anyway... we hope," Amy said.

"Oh sure, most of 'em do," said the old lady. "This'd be yours in here," she entered the last door on the left.

Amy, surprised at the unusual layout of the room, stepped through a small bathroom, then through another doorway into the large bedroom. The walls were all rich knotty pine with antiques everywhere. A beautiful queen size brass bed, obviously an antique, was on the left. The bed was so high they would need to use the little stool kept under it to get in. The pillows were stacked even higher and there was a small basket containing fruit, chocolate, a bottle of wine, and two glasses in the middle of the thick, old fashioned quilt.

Their hostess spoke in a soft voice as she nodded toward the basket on the bed, "That's Pierre's idea. After all these years he's still a romantic." She gave the room a quick glance as if checking to see all was as welcoming as she wanted.

Amy overcame her initial curiosity about the room's entrance being backward and said with a giggle, "Wow. What a nice room. Isn't this nice, Shawn?"

Shawn found a place to put down his oversized load of luggage and clothes and said, "Sure is, Amy. Yeah, real nice."

He asked, "How, I mean, why'd you put the bathroom here, though?"

The innkeeper said, "Well, we rent out five other rooms and some of 'em connect, ya know. We're still adding bathrooms." she pointed over to the corner where a door to another room was ajar.

"Oh, okay," Shawn said, "Just wondered. Yeah, nice in here, though. Very comfortable and homey."

They walked back out through the bathroom/entry and the proprietor said, "Well, do you need anything else? If you want something to eat the kitchen's open 'til twelve and the bar has snack food 'til one or so. It's right downstairs, you know? Just walk past the office and you're there."

Shawn and Amy looked at one another and then shook their heads no.

Amy said, "No, a snack later maybe, but nothing else that I can think of right now. Thanks. You need anything Shawn?"

"No, nothing for me. Just the room key, I guess."

The innkeeper looked at Shawn and said, "Oh, um, we leave the doors open all the time up here."

Amy and Shawn looked at each other and Shawn said, "Huh? You mean we leave the door unlocked? Even when we go sledding? I, ah…I don't know."

"Oh sure," the woman replied cheerfully, "Never had a problem. We're right down at the bottom of the steps, pret' near all the time, eh?"

Shawn figured they weren't going to install a lock tonight, and trying to find another room now was out of the question, so he said, "Well, okay. But you're sure everything is safe?"

"Well, you could take any serious money with you or we can put it in our safe downstairs. It'll be okay though, you'll see. Like I said, never had a problem, eh?"

Shawn shrugged and said, "All right I guess, we'll leave it unlocked."

"Sure, it'll be okay," said the old lady as she turned and started down the hall. "Just go ahead and leave it open. Good night now."

"Goodnight," Shawn and Amy in unison. They turned and passed through the bathroom and into the bedroom.

Shawn said, "What do ya think? You okay with this? Did you know about this deal?"

"Of course I didn't know. I guess it's okay. We didn't bring anything worth much, just a little cash. Just another reason to have left your pistol where it was though."

Amy's 'I told you so' was not lost on Shawn and he quickly added, "And you wouldn't sleep better if I had it? I know I would. That's three times today having it would've made me feel better."

"We'll block the door closed tonight, somehow," Amy said as she looked back into the bathroom. "I'm thinking more about someone that's been drinking too much walking in on me while I'm in the bathroom. That's more likely to happen than anybody stealing stuff."

Shawn shrugged and walked over to close the door in the corner but before he did he opened it wide and exposed the interior of the other room. He spied a crossed pair of feet on an ottoman but could only hear someone snoring softly.

As he quietly closed the door, he said to Amy in a whisper, "Damn, this one doesn't have a lock either. There's somebody sleeping in the room next door."

"No kiddin', Shawn? Remember, they rent out these rooms. Just put a chair in front of it. Here," she said as she took a ladder back chair from in front of the desk and propped it up under the doorknob. "There, done. How 'bout bringing in the rest of our stuff tomorrow? I'd like to get a piece of pie or something and some decaf. You want something?"

Shawn cocked his head sideways and said softly "Yeah, I want *something*," and moved closer to Amy.

Amy frowned and said, "You *are* kidding, right, bucco? After this day? The way it's been? I don't think so, dear. I need some food—*only* food—and now would be a good time."

Shawn hated it when Amy wasn't in the mood. It seemed to him that everything had to be perfect, in some specific order for her to want to do it. If she was tired, or cold, or sad, or if anything had upset her day, she was not the least bit interested, especially lately. They had some sex since his return, but for him it was never enough. He didn't want her to go downstairs to the bar alone so he reluctantly agreed and they went into the hall and closed the door tightly. As they passed the next room, Shawn glanced in to see if the guy was still sleeping. He was and the snoring was even louder than before.

Shawn said to Amy, "I guess we've got the better room. That one had the sink stuck right on the wall in the back corner. I wonder where the head is. Weird place, huh?"

Amy, walking toward the staircase, responded, "It's an old place, Shawn. Just a neat, old hotel. Let's just enjoy it for what it is, okay?"

They walked past the office and the room opened up into a sizable lounge area. A large number of snowmobilers had made their way to the Inn. Helmets and gloves were scattered everywhere. There were a number of people talking fairly loudly. They weren't rowdy but it was pretty evident they were having fun. There was laughter and an occasional shout. There was a fifties-style jukebox, just like the one Shawn and Amy had in their game room at home. It was lit up and pumping out the old song 'Bottle of Wine' over the huge speaker. An electric shuffleboard game was along the right wall with five or six men gathered around, taunting each other.

A small fire glowed in the cobblestone fireplace in the corner, heat radiating from the knee high hearth. Amy's eyes went directly to the mounted cougar above the fireplace, and then into the dining room beyond where perhaps dozens of stuffed animals, including another little black bear cub, lined the walls. There were chest height round tables near the fireplace. They found an empty one and sat down just outside the bar area.

Shawn said, "Neat."

Amy responded, "Yeah, but loud. I can't stay down here too long… I'll get a headache."

A waitress came to the table and asked what they would be drinking.

Amy smiled and said, "A cup of decaf, please. It has to be fresh, though, nothing that's been sitting around all night, okay?"

"Oh sure. No problem. Fresh it is. .And you, sir? Molson's our special tonight."

"Oh, just make it two, please. Decaf …And do you still have pie or dessert?"

"I'll check," the waitress said as she finished writing down the coffee order. She turned and walked past the stuffed rattlesnake coiled on the mantle and back into the kitchen.

She returned in a few minutes with the steaming coffee already poured in the large mugs and said, "Only thing left is some Crème Brule and Tiramisu."

Amy said, "I'll take the Tiramisu. I'm impressed; I didn't think you'd have that kind of dessert here."

Shawn added quickly, "Crème Brule for me please. I love that stuff."

The waitress said, "Must be your first time here. Are ya staying with us? We have a French pastry chef now. We do a lot of food business here, especially on weekends. Did you guys make dinner reservations for Friday and Saturday night? You need to 'cause we get filled up fast. Big dining room but it fills up fast."

"It's our first time up. We haven't made reservations but I guess we'd better," Amy said.

"If you want I can put you in now."

"Oh, okay, great! Kaan for both nights I guess," she looked toward Shawn for approval. "Better make it late, though, 'cause we'll be out riding a lot, we hope. Maybe seven-ish?"

"Okay, I'll mark ya down. I'll get your desserts," she walked back to the kitchen, stopping at several other tables along the way.

While they enjoyed their fantastic desserts, Shawn and Amy talked over the day's events. They were both relieved they were finally at their destination. They reiterated to one another their own view of all that had transpired and shared the hope that the rest of the trip would go more as planned and without anymore 'snags,' as Shawn called them.

Amy stated they would have plenty to tell their friends when they saw them at the next local snowmobile ride and, again mentioned their dear friend Bill and how he would have reacted to all they experienced today. Amy and Shawn both knew that even as big as he was, he would have been petrified with the storm and the fight.

Shawn said, "One thing for sure, we would still be out on the trail trying to find someone to ask directions if Bill had been riding with us."

Amy laughed and agreed, recalling when he must have stopped six times to "double check" on some directions he received along an unfamiliar trail they were riding. He always seemed so uncertain.

The hour passed quickly and they both drank too many cups of the best decaf coffee Amy had ever tasted. It had grown steadily noisier in the bar and they decided to call it a night. They paid their bill and walked slowly past the check in area and up the wide stairs to their room.

When they reached the bathroom-entry Amy said to Shawn, "Go ahead. I'll freshen up and see you in that wonderful, big brass bed."

Shawn had given up on having sex tonight. He didn't want to appear eager so he just nodded and closed the door behind him. It must have been that great dessert and coffee, he figured.

When Amy came out of the bathroom, Shawn's eyes lit up; she was wearing only her cotton panties. Shawn could tell from her erect nipples that she was either excited at the thought of having sex, or she was really, *really* cold. He didn't care what the reason. He was instantly ready. Amy stepped up on the stool and then hopped onto the high bed. As she nestled under the heavy, handmade quilt Shawn ducked into the bathroom to relieve himself and brush his teeth.

A few minutes later he emerged after quietly propping the plunger under the first panel in the hallway door. He turned off the bathroom light.

As he closed the bedroom door, he heard what he thought was the guy next door snoring louder than ever. But, as he climbed up onto the tall bed, it became more apparent it was Amy; something she didn't do very often.

Shawn tried to bounce around a bit, making as much noise as he thought he needed to wake her without getting her upset but to no avail. He went as far as a slight elbow in the back, and even rested his warm hand gently on her right breast, but it didn't work. He couldn't understand how she could pass up sex for sleep and even thought... well, maybe... since *he was so* ready... nah, she would wake up in the middle of it and really rip him apart. He would try to lie still awhile and unwind... but he sure could have used the stress relief that sex with Amy brought.

As Shawn lay next to Amy he began to notice music filtering through the floor. It seemed to be getting louder; boomba, boomba, boomba. Since his hearing had started to fail he couldn't recognize the music or hear any words, but it had a steady, rhythmic beat. He realized they were in the rear of the building, just above the bar. The old jukebox and the shouting and yelling were worrisome. What if some drunken mountain man decided to whip out a .357 and start shooting up the place... and them in the bed above it all?

As exhausted as he was, it still took a good half hour to fall asleep, hoping all along that Amy would regain consciousness and be up for the sex she more or less agreed to by being half naked.

Shawn had been asleep for about four hours when Amy awakened him. She was wrapping herself all around him. He thought about the promised sex and felt himself getting erect, only to hear Amy mumble that she was freezing. Shawn realized something was wrong when he felt

111

her shaking body. Light spilling in the nearby window allowed Shawn to see his breath.

He said to Amy, "What's wrong, babe?" He quickly added, "The heat must've gone off in the room," and jumped out of bed.

This had happened at home once before. The furnace went out during a frigid January night and fortunately the extreme cold woke Amy from a deep sleep before the pipes had time to freeze.

Shawn was shivering and moved swiftly around the dark room looking for the thermostat. He couldn't locate it. He told Amy to close her eyes and turned on the overhead light. He remembered electric baseboard heaters often have regulators on the ends of each unit. He noticed a quarter inch of ice had built up on the inside of the single pane window.

He turned toward Amy and asked, "Amy, did that old lady say, 'Leave the door unlocked?' or did she say, 'Leave the door open?'"

Amy didn't respond and Shawn repeated, this time louder, "Amy! I said did that lady tell us to leave the door opened up or just unlocked?"

Amy mumbled, "Open, she said *open.* Turn it on, Shawn. I'm freezing."

Shawn said nothing as he passed through the bathroom, knocked the plunger out of the way with his foot and opened the hallway door. The light was on in the hall and he immediately felt the warm air flowing around him and moving back into their room. It was then he spied the ten-foot long electric baseboard heater in the hallway.

"It's out here, Amy. The damned heater is in the stupid hallway. That's why they want us to leave the doors open. This is great, just great. No security *and* no heat."

He re-entered the bathroom without closing the door and left the bedroom door wide open, as well. He hopped back into bed and started to feel warm air on his face. Under the covers, however, it was still very cold.

"It must be twenty degrees, Shawn," Amy was still shaking. "I'm dying here, bucco."

Shawn said, "I know. Me too." He climbed back out of bed. He unzipped one of the duffels they had brought and sorted through it. He pulled out two pairs of silk underwear they wore while snowmobiling.

"Here, put these on," he tossed them under the quilt.

Shawn opened the train case on the floor and slid his hand along the wall on Amy's side of the bed. She heard him fumble with the wall plug and then heard a loud noise. She felt warm air as Shawn slid the Con Air hair dryer, now on high, under her side of the quilt. Instantaneous warmth! They used the hair dryer for only ten minutes because each time it overheated the dryer's breaker clicked off.

They hugged each other as they waited for it to cool down enough to turn back on. The third time it went off they were generating their own heat. The sex that had been promised turned out to be Shawn's reward for being innovative. It was one of the best ways they could think of to create a lot of heat.

First Full Day's Ride

Shawn was first to awaken; a combination of sunlight and voices from the hallway was the cause. He rolled over and looked at the clock radio beside the bed. Much to his surprise, the readout was 10:02 AM.

He blinked twice and then shook Amy from sleep.

He said softly, "Hey, Amy, it's after ten. We slept in."

Amy rolled over, looked at the clock and also heard the voices from the hallway.

She spoke with her eyes still closed, "Close the outside door. I'm not ready to get up yet."

Naked, he stepped down from the high bed. His back gave him a small twinge of pain, but not enough to slow his quick dash over to the icy window. He scraped at the glazing with his thumbnail and cleared a small circle so he could see outside. He gazed toward a tree covered hillside.

"Oh! Come on, Amy, look. It's beautiful out. Suns up. Let's eat a quick breakfast and ride."

With his face pressed up to the icy window he said, "Pretty here, Amy. Looks like it snowed a little more. Not that it needed it. Looks deep though," he said. "Lots of evergreens around. Lots of mountain laurel and stuff. Come on, get up. It's warmer in here now."

Amy sighed a little, like she did every Monday morning when she got up for work. She rolled over, rubbed her eyes and looked at the clock.

"Hey, it's after ten, Shawn. We slept really late."

Shawn nodded his head and said, "Yup. You want in the shower first?"

"Oh, no, go ahead, Shawn. You'll take longer. I'll wait here," she mumbled as she rolled back over.

"Maid service." came in loud and clear from the opened doorway to the hall.

"You up, eh?" the maid questioned.

She stood at the hallway door with a cleaning cart behind her; middle aged and heavy, wearing a black and white uniform and with her dark hair pulled tightly back and tied at the nape of her neck, she stared at Shawn with a disparaging look as he stood, still naked, in front of the frosted window.

Amy sat up and said, "No… *no.* We are not. We'll, we are… but come back later. *Please…* Thank you."

"Okay," the maid responded. "No problem. Later it is. But it's after ten now... But no problem, eh," she mumbled to herself but still loud enough for Shawn and Amy to hear. She took a final look back at Shawn, shook her head and began to lumber down the hallway.

Amy said in a snappy tone mimicking the maids accent, "Good, a no a perobilem then a… eh?"

Shawn aimed a curious look at Amy who was sitting bolt up-right in bed, and started for the outside door.

He shouted at the maid's stiffly retreating form, "But, hey, thanks! Ah, we'll be out soon…'bout half an hour."

"I told you to close that door, Shawn." Amy slipped back down on her pillow.

"Yeah, but you shouldn't be so abrupt, Amy. She was only trying to do her job."

"Good. Let her do it later. I'm busy right now," Amy said as she closed her eyes mumbling, "Besides, I can be nasty if I want to, I haven't had my coffee yet."

Before he left for Iraq, even in the summers when he was off from school, Shawn was always the first one up. He would grind and brew a pot of coffee and take a cup in to Amy while she was still in bed. He hadn't missed a morning since they had been married and often thought she was really getting spoiled. He had noticed lately, though, she didn't seem to be able to focus clearly without coffee first thing in the morning. Maybe she was right. Maybe she had just been sleepy when she called him Brad.

Shawn remembered it was he who got her started on the coffee habit and said, "I'll get your coffee first and then I'll take my shower."

He quickly pulled on a pair of underwear and then blue jeans and his favorite Marco Island sweatshirt he had bought near Uncle Bud's place in Florida.

"I'll be right back," giving her a quick kiss on the cheek.

When he walked out of the room he left the outer door half open.

"*Close it!*" Amy directed him.

Two seconds later, a slight "click" could be heard.

When Shawn went downstairs there was no one around. It was silent and void of life. It looked very different from the packed, bustling place they experienced last night.

He stood at the door to the kitchen and called out in a soft tone, "Hello? Hello. Anyone here?"

Silence.

"Hel-lo-o…Anyone here?" he spoke louder into the continued silence.

"Hey! Anybody up yet?" he bellowed.

"Oh, *you,* eh?" came the reply as the large maid came lumbering around the silver walk-in cooler. "I do room now?"

"Oh, uh, no, not yet," Shawn stammered, "We just wanted to get some coffee. Or is there room service?"

The woman looked Shawn up and down, much as she had in the bedroom and said, "No, no room service. No."

"Well then, I'll just pick up some coffee."

"No, no, we have no coffee yet. No one here to do it. Coffee…not 'til eleven or so…Lunchtime cook comes in at eleven…Not 'til then…Come back then."

"Okay… How 'bout some instant coffee and some hot water," Shawn suggested.

"Nope," she replied, "No instant here…This a good restaurant. Nothing instant, eh? Nope."

Shawn realized that the maid could be upset because of Amy's bitchy attitude earlier. He decided to try using some charm. Maybe it would work for him as well as it did for Amy when she wanted something from some guy.

He leaned against the doorway and crossed his right foot over his left as the maid continued to stare at him. He said with a wink, "I'm sure you've got ways of makin' things hot back there," he nodded toward the gas stove.

The maid looked Shawn in the eye and said, "You been sick? Pretty skinny, eh? You need to pack on some meat an' come back then. Nope, nuttin' hot back here."

Shawn was slightly embarrassed that his machismo method had gotten him nowhere with this old behemoth. And he was very aware that he now had to face Amy without any coffee.

"Well, if it was really a good restaurant, you'd not only have coffee, you'd have room service."

He believed Amy would be proud to hear him assert himself this way. At this point he figured it didn't really matter if the room got cleaned or not.

"Go across street. Gas station has machine. Not good but hot, eh?"

"Thanks." with a smile. He turned and headed quickly out the front door.

After he left the inn, he realized how cold it was outside but didn't want to go back to the room to get a coat without coffee, so he toughed it out. He was lucky; the sun helped make the 20 degree temperature more tolerable. After his tour in the 'oven' of Iraq, Shawn had found it more difficult to tolerate the cold.

As he started back across the street, Shawn had to wait for some snowmobiles to pass. There was a group of about ten who looked prepared for a long ride. All the sleds had packs strapped to the rear racks; an indication these riders were on an overnight trip. Shawn knew some riders would travel over a thousand miles in a little more than a week in this kind of environment. One of the older snowmobiles in the group was emitting some smoke and Shawn arrived at the room smelling like burnt motor oil.

He knocked and Amy unblocked the door. He entered the bathroom as Amy stepped back behind the steamy shower curtain.

"Boy, you messing around with the sleds already? You smell smoky."

"Nah, I had to go across the street to get the coffee. No one works here until lunch. The coffee might be a little cool; I had to wait for sleds in the street. There's a ton of people out riding already."

"Good! You ready to get in the shower? I'll let this run 'cause it's good and hot now. It was cold for a long time at first."

"Yeah, sure, I'll be right in," yelled Shawn stepping into the bedroom. He took a big gulp of his rapidly cooling coffee and then shed his clothes. "Hey, why didn't we think of hot showers last night, Amy? We could have slept in a virtual hot tub."

"Yeah, and drowned. Who do you know that has ever slept in a bathtub, Shawn?"

"I did. I did it sometimes when I was a kid. But only on cold mornings."

"Huh? Why did'ja do that?" Amy questioned between sips of lukewarm coffee as she dried off.

Shawn slipped into the shower and said, "Well, you recall the old house I grew up in? The bedrooms were on the second floor and the bathroom in the basement, remember that?"

"Yeah, strange setup but I think a lot of real old houses were like that then."

"Well," Shawn continued. "We had a little gas heater in there in the winter time and it would be the warmest place in the house, warmer than my bedroom, for sure."

"Yeah... So?"

"Well, my mom would wake me up early for school and I'd trudge through the rest of the cold house, downstairs to the basement and when I'd hit that warm bathroom, oh man, I'd get *so* sleepy again."

"Okay, I think I might, too. So what? What about the tub?"

Shawn said, "Well the tub was that big old cast iron claw foot that I wanted to bring to our house when Dad sold the place, remember? It would be just cooking, right beside the gas heater. I'd get cleaned up real quick using the sink and then throw a rolled up bath towel on the back of the tub, climb in and catch another forty winks; just for fifteen minutes or so, or until my Mom would start yelling, 'Shawn, you're gonna be late! You'll miss the bus!'"

"I'd wake up, scramble up to my room, get dressed and off to school I'd go! Probably did that a couple dozen times or so. Just in really cold weather. Ha, ha, neat, huh?"

Amy tried to smother the laughter she was holding back.

"Shawn, you *weirdo!*" she laughed out loud. "That's the strangest thing I've ever heard. You're a sicky, you really are."

Shawn said proudly and a little stiffly, "I think it was pretty inventive. Not to mention restful. It's what sets me apart from the average thinker."

"Yeah, okay. You're set apart from any thinker, bucco," Amy laughed as she went into the bedroom. She stopped and looked back into the bathroom and added, "And I don't want to hear any snoring coming from this bathroom, either."

"Yeah, yeah, yeah," Shawn replied to a now empty room. He had questioned himself as to that being the very beginning of his back problems but ruled it out.

Amy reappeared in the bedroom doorway and said, "Hey, Shawn, did ya ever think that might have caused some of your back problems? Really?"

"Don't be silly, Amy, no, it did not. But thank you."

Since no breakfast could be had at the inn, the plan was to munch on granola bars Amy had packed in the duffle as a trail meal, unload the snowmobiles and ride some place for an early lunch/late breakfast. By the time they finished getting dressed and unloaded the sleds they found they could have eaten at the inn after all. They decided against it as a protest for not getting the coffee and food they expected first thing in the morning.

After they started their snowmobiles and allowed them to warm up, Shawn looked over the local map he had obtained the week before. He had encased it in plastic and mounted it on the XMZ fuel tank map pocket. He had made himself familiar with the surrounding area by reading the map and memorizing the parts that seemed the most important.

"Amy, we'll go across this lake and run over to the restaurant. It's between the two lakes. It should be well marked. It's on the main blue trail. Then we'll see from there," he pointed at a dot on the map and shouted over the rumbling engines.

Amy nodded and turned her sled away from the main lodge toward the white lake about a hundred feet away. She could barely see the other side and had hoped their first trip wouldn't be across the entire lake; but it was going to be. Shawn pulled alongside Amy and glanced over to see if she was ready. She checked her fuel gauge and signaled to Shawn that it was full with a "thumbs-up."

They approached the shoreline with some trepidation. But the lakes here freeze deeply and are approved for riding, not like at home. Shawn and Amy could tell, as they rode out onto the snow covered ice, that the lake was solidly frozen. The sleds had feedback through the handlebars, a slightly hollow, drumming vibration when the ice was thin or unstable. This time there was none of that, not even a hint they had left firm ground just a short acceleration away from the old boat dock on shore.

They were by no means alone on the lake. There were men ice fishing just off-shore. They made the trek back and forth on snowmobiles or hand pulled sleds. There were a wide variety of 4x4s parked out as far as the middle of the lake. Shawn even spotted another military Hum-Vee next to a tent. If he lived here that is what he would drive.

The late morning was calm, sunny and beautiful. Shawn had been right when he thought there had been a light snowfall during the night. The storm of the night before had covered all the old tracks. They had ridden lakes before and knew to follow the tree limbs carefully stuck upright in mounds of snow every quarter mile or so.

They cruised comfortably at about fifty miles an hour and when they reached the center of the lake, they saw a lot more activity. They could see about a ten mile area and there were several more temporary fishing villages. Individuals were arriving on sleds, there were groups of parked sleds, cross country skiers and even an airplane fitted with skis. People were moving in all directions or sitting by the holes cut in the ice for fishing.

All the activity was a bit unsettling for Shawn but he soon realized the chance of any kind of problem was very unlikely and he soon relaxed and began to enjoy the ride.

Shawn was very aware that they were riding on frozen water and was constantly watching for signs of thinning ice or open water areas. He regularly stood on the running boards to look for anything that was different from the surrounding surface: dark, shiny or slushy places indicated a possible breach in the integrity of the ice.

One thing a snowmobiler must never do is slow down in such a place. The heavy sleds can stay afloat but only as long as there is forward momentum. An abrupt turn or going too slowly would be disastrous. The best advice Shawn had been able to get was to keep the throttle wide open and sail over the slushy spots, or even open water if they encountered any. He and Amy had rehearsed what to do if that should happen, but neither of them really expected to have to use the technique.

Shawn remembered the times he and Amy and some of their friends were riding on lakes around western New York. Their friend, Sno-mo Bill, had a real fear of plunging through the ice. One summer, at a winter trip planning get-together, Bill questioned why no one had ever invented a type of life vest a snowmobiler could wear under his suit to keep him afloat if he ever went into the water. No one could think of why it wouldn't work and the subject was dropped. It came up again the next winter trip to Lake Chautauqua when Bill was having a steering problem during the ride. Shawn helped fix the problem in the hotel parking lot before the second day's ride.

When Shawn went into Bill's SUV for some tools he noticed three or four bicycle inner tubes lying out in the open. Shawn couldn't imagine what the bicycle tubes were for as he had never seen Bill on a bicycle. This must be his new safety device.

As he handed Bill the tools he poked him in the stomach and said, "Do they work, or did you just gain a little weight this fall?"

Bill quickly glanced at the open truck with a nonplussed expression on his face.

"Won't know 'til I get wet... Right?"

Shawn realized Bill would not appreciate being chided and chose not to pursue it.

"Well, let's hope that never happens."

That weekend it did, however. Not to Bill but to several young local snowmobilers.

The day after discovering Bill's safety apparatus, Shawn's group was out riding at the north end of the lake. A large red and white Coast Guard helicopter kept circling at low altitude. A Sheriff's deputy stopped their group at an intersection, asking if they had seen a young couple in their early twenties riding on a single sled. The girl was wearing a hot pink jacket and gloves. No one had. He said if they did see them, to have the couple check back with their relatives as soon as possible, they were worried about them.

A short time later they were having lunch at a restaurant on the far side of the lake. A man entered who was searching for the couple. He went from table to table asking if anyone had seen the people in his pictures; he was concerned as to the whereabouts of his sister and her boyfriend.

They were riding double on his sled and had been part of a fifty mile night ride from the snowmobile clubhouse to this very restaurant last night. They never arrived home and no one had seen them. There were about a hundred riders and, after eating, the couple decided to head back early. They left with one other rider The trip to the restaurant took four hours on the trails but they apparently chose the faster way back; across the lake. Unfortunately, they chose to start across at a boat ramp located near a feeder canal and the ice was too thin to support the weight of the sleds.

All three were located two days later when another rider entered the same spot during daylight and also plunged into the icy water. He was lucky, however. His partners held back when he went onto the lake, concerned it was thin, snow-covered ice. They were able to pull him safely to shore. When they did, someone noticed a hot pink glove bob to the surface in the slushy mix. It was the young girl's glove released from under the frozen surface, sending an eerie signal as to where to find the bodies.

Shawn and Amy were at home when Bill called with the terrible news of the find. He had been so concerned he checked with the Sheriff's office a few days later and they related the sad story. Bill never did go back out onto a lake or even want to cross over streams after that experience. As for Shawn, he never again brought up what he thought was Bill's peculiar habit of wearing bicycle inner tubes under his suit. He now realized it could have been a life saving answer to a desperate safety concern.

Shawn snapped back to the present when a sled zoomed past them at about 80 miles per hour.

On a large lake it is normal to be passed by someone riding faster. There is very little warning since the other rider is coming from behind. It is good riding etiquette to allow plenty of room, but Shawn was still startled. He realized he had been daydreaming again.

"Wow," Shawn said out loud as the sled made a large arc to the left and soon disappeared in the distance.

"Couldn't make out what that was," he said as if talking to Amy.

Then Shawn shook his head and mumbled "Stupid" to himself. He had forgotten that he and Amy had decided to forego their radios on this trip. The headsets added several pounds to their already heavy helmets and, unless they were riding with a large group, they didn't normally use them. The radios were handy to communicate a warning about a dangerous area or stopping for a break. Shawn thought maybe tomorrow they would use them since there was so much to see.

Large lake shorelines all look alike in the snow, but Shawn had an uncanny ability to find a landing area from which to exit a lake. He was able to steer right to the spot where other sleds safely negotiated access to the shore. Shawn just kept his eyes open. He had learned that sooner or later, a preponderance of tracks built a curve leading to the safest exit point at the shoreline. If he was first in line, he could usually see tracks that curved toward shore, indicating where to leave the frozen lake surface.

He noticed the fast moving sled that had just passed them taking a turn towards shore and began to watch for the telltale signs in the snow. Sure enough, a number of tracks curved to the exit where a small amount of disturbed brown earth was showing.

As Shawn approached the shore and slowed for the exit he heard a loud cracking sound from the ice. He squeezed the throttle just a little. He wanted only enough speed to carry him onto the shore, stopping about ten yards beyond the lake's edge. He never liked the sound the ice made as it flexed under the weight of the sleds.

The ice highway used by truckers in the northern reaches of Canada is the example Shawn emulated. As heavily loaded eighteen-wheeled, tractor-trailer trucks cross frozen lakes, the ice actually bends under their weight. If the truck is going too fast when it approaches the area near the shoreline, the ripples created under the ice will actually arrive first and explode into the air, sinking the truck before it can reach the shoreline.

He shut off his engine as he again recalled the young couple who had drowned.

He turned to Amy and said, "You hear that, Amy?"

"Yeah, always scares me, Shawn," Amy responded as she turned off her sled and lifted her face shield. "I always think about that girl and her friends in New York."

"Me, too, but you know it always moves around a little. It's plenty thick enough around here…The ice."

"Yeah, I know, but after that deal I've always been a little nervous. I don't know how you find the exit on a new lake…You amaze me sometimes, Shawn."

127

"Me, too. I amaze me, too." he said with a smile. "I think the restaurant is just off this trail," he added quickly so Amy didn't ask about his simple system of appearing so knowledgeable.

"I hope so; I'm getting really hungry now."

They started their sleds again and entered the tree line. They saw a small hand painted "EAT" sign not an eighth of a mile up the trail and turned off to the right.

They rode the country road for about two miles until they arrived at a small store, gas station and restaurant combination. They parked their sleds in front and pulled the keys out of the ignition. The restaurant was almost full of snowmobilers and was loud with chatter. The smell of bacon and coffee wafted through the air. Amy and Shawn found a booth open and sat down, placing their helmets alongside them on the seats.

A waitress appeared almost instantly and said, "Yunz want coffee this morning?"

"You're from Pittsburgh, aren't you?" Amy asked and nodded yes for coffee.

"Yep. Yunz?" as she poured steaming hot coffee to the rim.

"Grew up there but moved away. Always miss it though."

"How'd ya know I was from the 'burgh?" the waitress asked.

"It's the 'yunz'. Ha, it's the 'yunz', yinz use," Shawn said smiling.

"Oh, yeah, right." the waitress responded. "Ferget that sometimes gives it away," she laughed. "Still love 'em Stillers though. Yunz want a menu? We got a omelet special," she said to Amy as she looked back over her shoulder at people leaving. A seasoned waitress, Amy thought.

"Sure do," Amy replied. "And some water, too, please."

"Amy, don't drink too much water, though, okay? Long ride today," Shawn said.

The waitress, bonding with Amy and coming to her aid, immediately said to Shawn, "You let her drink it. You'll have bad kidneys someday, but she'll be fine."

"Yeah, yeah, heard it all before," Shawn said. "I'm just not sure where the stops are yet…We just got here."

"Oh yeah? Where yunz stayin'?"

Shawn never liked to give out too much information and just said, "Down the lake a bit."

Amy, happy that she had made a new friend so quickly, added, "The Westside Inn."

After she handed the menus over the waitress said, "Yeah, nice place Westside. Sleep there yet?"

Shawn and Amy, sipping hot coffee, accepted the menus with one hand and manage a simultaneous, " Uh huh."

"Sleep with your suits on… or suits off?" the waitress questioned.

Instantly, Shawn and Amy thought of their night and sprayed a fine mist of coffee toward the table as they tried to control their laughter. Wiping coffee off their faces with their napkins, they began to laugh out loud.

The waitress added, "Yeah, most out-of-towner's don't know about the heat. We hear about it every year so it's a big joke 'round here. Known fact, no one 'round here stays over in the winter unless they have their snowmobile suits on. Just wondrin'," she smiled and winked at them over her shoulder as she turned and walked to another table.

Amy and Shawn settled back and smiled while looking over the menus.

Shawn said with a chuckle, "Maybe we should look at it like an initiation or something. You know, 'Welcome to the Ice Side Inn.' Or 'Come to the Westside Icehouse.'"

"Yeah, a free hair dryer in every bed." added Amy.

They laughed and selected the fare that appealed to them this morning. It would be oatmeal and brown sugar for Amy and a ham and cheese omelet with home fries, toast, and bacon for Shawn. He claimed he ate pretty well in Iraq—when he could—but there was something special about American food, or in this case *North* American food, that he couldn't pass up.

"Hey, how about those fishing villages out there, Amy?" Shawn said.

"Yeah, I'm amazed they put all that stuff so close together. And the trucks."

"I bet that ice is over a foot thick. It would have to be to hold that many vehicles, huh?"

A man seated at the next booth turned around and said, "It's close to two feet out in the middle, maybe more. If you want to be accurate just ask the fishermen. They know the exact thickness. They have to drill it." he laughed.

"Yeah, good point there, thanks," Shawn said.

Amy added, "And the planes. I've never seen that many airplanes on a lake at one time."

The man responded, "That's how we get around up here. For some places, that's the only way to get in. Lots of cabins and houses out there on the edges of the lakes or on the islands. With those skis on the planes they never have a problem. They're light, too. Now the trucks do go in once in a while... I can tell you that from personal experience."

Shawn said, "You mean you actually lost a vehicle in the water?"

"Oh, yeah. I was on a large float that broke away one spring out on the big lake. After the wind picked up it took about five hours to get rescued. But my truck went down with fifteen others. Still down there, I guess. I didn't want them to dry it out and give it back to me, that's for sure," he laughed.

Amy said, "I never thought about it before. Could you feel the float moving?"

"Oh yeah. It was a lot like being on a huge barge. You could feel it riding the waves. And it was moving pretty good. When they picked us up we were about two miles downwind. It was very... well, interesting," he turned back around.

"I'll bet," said Shawn. "Yeah, that *is* interesting... Thanks."

After they finished their hearty breakfast they used the bathroom. Shawn was disappointed the locals didn't seem to adhere to the exchange rate in the way he expected. Breakfast was twenty six American dollars, a sum that Shawn thought exorbitant in any country. He vowed the tip would now be less, even if he liked the service. Amy, on the other hand, never complained about the cost of any part of her vacation. She figured if you started to worry about the nickels and dimes, you wouldn't enjoy yourself.

They donned their helmets as they waited for the idling sleds to warm up.

Amy pulled out first and stopped before crossing the main road. Shawn quickly passed Amy and they entered the woods on a remarkably smooth and wide trail. Shawn slowed enough for Amy to catch up and they whisked up a long winding slope and into the dark green pine forest.

They had the good fortune to be the first riders on the groomed trail. It was a rare treat to fly over the smooth surface and they both laughed out loud as they sped along. They hummed along at 35 miles per hour and barely had to slow to take the large bends around the pines and hardwoods. It allowed both of them to steer more by shifting their weight than by turning the handlebars. This heavenly ride lasted for about forty minutes.

They encountered only two other riders on the trail. They were headed in the opposite direction and after taking a sharp left turn they saw the groomer parked on the left side of the trail. It had the right side jacked up, the track splayed open front to back. As they approached Shawn saw that the operator was lying on his side, struggling to work a bottle jack with his right arm.

Shawn pulled to the right, well off the trail and signaled for Amy to do the same. As he dismounted and stepped from the snowmobiles running board he sank up to his knees in soft snow. It took a few seconds to drag himself back up onto the trail. He removed his helmet and placed it on his sled's seat, and walked toward the groomer's operator.

"Need some help?" Shawn said to the large man dressed in coveralls, now rolled over on his back.

"Ah, sure, hand me that spanner wrench on the cab step, eh?" the man replied as he changed positions so that he was kneeling in front of a tire.

Shawn handed the guy the wrench and he grunted and tugged on one of three wheels with a funny looking, thick tire on it. He managed to remove it and Shawn got ready to take it, but the guy just got up and with one motion, threw the wheel and tire into an open chest bolted to the hood.

"Flat," he said. "But no problem, eh? Got another right here," as he rolled one from the back of the Bombi groomer.

Shawn couldn't tell the difference between the good one and the one that had just been removed but he nodded his agreement anyway. In a matter of minutes Shawn and the man were re-attaching the track over the new wheel and tire. Amy stood back and recorded Shawn's efforts on her camera phone. She knew Shawn would brag to his buddies that he saved all of "snowmobile-dom" from bumpy trails this trip. She would have the proof he might require.

When the two men finished the repair, the operator used waterless soap to clean his hands and then lit a cigarette.

"Happens every couple weeks on these," he said looking toward the Bombi. "You get a leaker and all of a sudden it won't turn or track straight, nuthin', eh? Pain in the butt. Oughta make 'em outta sumpin' solid, eh?"

Shawn began to answer his comment while the operator stared back with a quizzical look on his face. Shawn talked about the physics involved when subjecting natural rubber products to extremely cold temperatures. Suddenly he noticed Amy shaking her head side to side.

He stopped and said, "Yeah, you're right, they ought to…um…We're supposed to pay you for the trail permit I think," Shawn said as he started to unzip his jacket pocket for some money.

"Nah, not after gettin' me out of a jam, you're not," said the operator. "Anyone asks you for a permit, tell 'em Tom took care of it. They'll know what you mean, eh?"

"Oh, well, you sure, um, Tom? I've got it right here. No problem."

"Nope!" said Tom emphatically. "And if I were you, I'd be ridin' my sled on the blue trail after noon today. And the yellow trail first thing in the mornin' cause that's where I'll be groomin'… Barring any more flats, that is!"

"Great, Tom, and thanks. We really appreciate it. And the trails are just fantastic. Best we've ever ridden on."

"Good. That's why we do it, eh?" Tom shouted as he climbed up the step and into the cab. "See ya, now," he said as he started the Bombi's diesel engine, sending up a puff of sooty, black smoke from the big exhaust pipe. He engaged the clutch, inched forward and steered out onto the trail, the yellow strobe light flashing. Halting beside Shawn, he hollered down from the cab window, "That's a lot better, thanks for your help, ah, ah."

"Oh, it's Shawn. I'm Shawn Kaan, that's Amy," motioning back behind him.

"Hey, take the green trail up ahead a mile or so. It's not too bad and you won't need to follow me," he waved his good-bye as he pulled out.

He slid the cab window closed with a thunk and sped away, much more swiftly and quietly than either Shawn or Amy expected.

Shawn made his way back toward his sled and wished Tom had noticed him sink to his knees in the soft snow in case he needed a tow. But as he climbed aboard his sled it felt like it was on solid footing. He applied the throttle sparingly and the sled pulled out without hesitation. He checked his mirrors and Amy was once again scooting along just behind him, acting like she was about to pass him. Within a few minutes they turned onto a large, smooth logging road with a green placard on the first large tree after the turn. They accelerated to about thirty or so and settled in for a relaxing ride toward the waterfall they had read about in a snowmobiling/travel magazine. *Tom was right*, Shawn thought, *it was a very smooth trail.*

After twenty-five minutes of non-stop riding, Shawn pulled off near a large intersection. He climbed off his sled to stretch. He and Amy sat side-saddle on the XMZ and talked about the scenery. Another sled pulled up across the intersection. It was one of the new, huge touring sleds Shawn had only seen pictures of and it carried a rider that must have weighed 400 pounds. In addition to the rider, it had a tent, a nap sack, snow shoes, snow skis and poles and what looked like a nine cubic foot food locker on board.

Amy giggled and said to Shawn, "Hey, I know that guy's name. It's Chuck. Yeah, that's it, Chuck. You know, for Chuck Wagon? He must have fifty pounds of food on there, huh?"

Shawn laughed and said, "He must be doing some serious camping up here. Probably on the trail a week or two. That'd be fun. I'd do it if I had the free time in the winter."

Amy said, "Not with me, though. Roughing it would be in a motorhome."

Shawn said, "Yeah, I guess he's got the same kind of wife I do. Must know how to cook well, though. Look how *huge* he is."

As the big sled glided past, they all exchanged nods and then Shawn and Amy climbed back onto their sleds. Shawn hesitated and suddenly got back off. He walked to Amy and indicated she should take the XMZ; he would ride her sled for awhile. At first, Amy resisted because she didn't like to ride a big heavy sled; plus, they didn't own it. She also wasn't fond of anyone else riding her sled—even Shawn—he had a tendency to treat it rougher than Amy did. Then she caved, walked up to Shawn's snowmobile and climbed aboard.

As long as she was up front already, she figured she would just stay there. Before Shawn was ready, she flew across the intersection and down the trail. It was graded in such a way as to have gradual curves and Amy could travel at a high rate of speed, fishtailing each time she cracked open the throttle.

It didn't take long for Shawn to get nervous and pass her. He pulled over to the side of the trail. They didn't even look at one another as they switched sleds and remounted. Shawn led at a more respectable pace.

They were disappointed with the waterfall—which turned out to be two, five-foot-high falls spewing root beer colored water. Although they were about one hundred feet wide, the smelly water and the less than breathtaking height seemed a little anti-climatic; certainly not the way the magazine made it sound. Upstream, however, they happened onto several large isolated, frozen lakes and had some fun chasing each other in large circles out in the middle.

Shawn, swooping near the far end of the lake, saw a large green and yellow cage-like object protruding out of the frozen water. He pulled to within ten feet, dismounted and leaving the engine idling, casually strolled up to a pipe railing and peered down into a ten-foot deep hole. The sound of rushing water filtered through his helmet's closed face shield. He studied the water flow for a few seconds, wondering about the reason for the running water and the steel pipe structure.

Suddenly, Shawn felt his stomach tighten and he grabbed the pipe handrail with both hands. He realized he was perched on the lip of an automatic spillway that controlled the water level for the lake. He saw something else that really scared him; the surface of the water had been lowered and was at least ten feet below where he stood. If the ice gave way and he was to fall in he would never be able to climb back out. He thought of crawling slowly back from the edge of the abyss but the fear was too great; he simply made a run for it. He lunged for his sled and cracked the throttle wide open. The sled's carbide picks dug into the ice and the skis lifted high in the air. Shawn held on, his knees just grazing the seat, as he sped away toward safety.

He flew past Amy, still accelerating and looking more like an Xtreme snowmobiler. He yelled at Amy to get off the lake. She couldn't understand what he was shouting and couldn't do anything quickly anyway; she was laughing too hard. She eventually followed Shawn onto land.

"What the hell's wrong with you, Shawn?" Amy laughed.

"Oh man, Amy. You don't know … That lake was *dropped* ten feet! We were on air! *Nothing* under the ice. It wasn't water, ya know, just air. They must have dropped the water level after it froze. Boy, we were so lucky. Wonder why no signs? We could've gone in." Shawn said, shaking his head from side to side.

"Boy, you'd never know from looking at it, huh? Well, we'll stay off these out of the way lakes from now on. No sense getting wet."

"Getting wet is not the worry, Amy. Ten feet. Did you hear me? *Ten feet!* You'd never be able to climb out of that. Whew."

"I never liked lakes much anyway, Shawn. I don't even want to know about the big one maybe being like that. So don't even ask anyone. Okay?"

"Okay. I don't want to know either, Amy. Let's just go back. Rest a bit and eat at the inn early… Wow," Shawn said as he started his sled.

Amy nodded and tried to start her sled. The starter made a grinding noise but the engine didn't fire. Usually it started the quickest. Not this time. She tried three more times and then smelled gasoline so she turned off the key and sat back.

Shawn looked over his shoulder and then started to move, expecting Amy to be ready. He stopped and watched her get off and open the hood. He turned his sled off.

"What's the matter?"

"I don't know, but I smell gas."

138

Shawn eyed the engine and pulled the emergency start rope. When he did gasoline pumped back out of the one carburetor. The more he pulled the more gasoline squirted out.

"Float must be stuck," Shawn said. "Probably when you hit that bump there," he pointed at the edge of the lake.

"Don't act like it's my fault, Shawn. You're the one that took off like an idiot," Amy responded in a defensive tone.

"I'm not blaming you, hun. These things happen."

"Don't 'hun' me now, Shawn. Just fix it, ok?"

"I will if I can," Shawn fired back.

He began tapping the float bowl with a screwdriver handle, trying to dislodge the float in its chamber. The first three hits didn't do any good, so he gave it a good firm whack ... and watched as the rest of the fuel in the bowl began to cascade over the lower part of the engine and onto the chassis. He had cracked the fuel bowl. That meant there was no way Amy's sled would be able to make the return trip under power.

"Oh man, damn it!" Shawn yelled and threw the screwdriver into the snow. "I can't believe this. We're screwed now, Amy. I'll have to tow it back."

"If we go back the way we came, it'll take us hours."

"Well, check the map, then. I think we can cut off some miles where we saw Chuck Wagon and get on the lake quicker. Towing on the lake will be easy. But out here on the trail, you know, it's gonna be a pain in the butt."

Amy opened the map while Shawn turned the fuel line valve off, removed the engine drive belt and carefully closed the hood of Amy's disabled snowmobile.

They connected the-six-foot, bungee-style towrope by hooking it to the front of each ski on Amy's sled and the rear bumper of Shawn's. Shawn reminded Amy to use the brake a little when going down hills, and not attempt to steer, the towrope would take care of that.

The ride back was not much of a problem for Shawn's powerful sled, but it was slow going around trees and tight corners. They turned where Shawn thought they should and he was right. Amy shook her head in relieved disbelief; it was uncanny how Shawn could find his way around, even in unknown territory.

When they approached the edge of the lake, Shawn stopped. He told Amy to get on behind him. He felt it would be safer because they would be traveling faster on the lake. Amy protested a little but knew Shawn was probably right.

Shawn planned to move rapidly on the lake. He was a little apprehensive about the weight of two sleds traveling so close together. While they rechecked the tow set-up, two young boys, neither wearing helmets, pulled up beside them on an antique snowmobile and shouted over an un-muffled engine.

"Hey, you goin' down the lake that way?" the young driver pointed the way they planned to go.

Shawn responded, "Yup. Why?"

The passenger answered, "We just heard someone went in down near LacDranna!"

"Are you sure?"

"Yup, hit slush… and drowned!"

Shawn and Amy just looked at each other, the memory of Bill's inner tubes running through their minds.

140

Shawn said, "Okay, thanks."

As the boys pulled away, Amy said, "What do you think, Shawn?"

Shawn looked down the lake and saw perhaps fifteen or twenty snowmobiles and fishing huts.

He said, "Nah, if we don't go we'll have to leave it and come back with the trailer. Look out there, it's gotta be safe. We'll be okay."

Amy nodded, snuggled up behind Shawn and put her arms around his waist. As they approached the lake, Shawn wanted to take no chances on the two sleds plunging into the water if the ice along the shoreline was thin. He gave it more throttle than Amy expected and the sleds rumbled onto the packed surface, accelerating hard. Amy was forced back and her boots started to leave the running boards. She squeezed Shawn around the middle with enough power to send a painful reminder that she was behind him—not on her sled. He got the message and eased off the throttle, settling into a more comfortable cruising speed.

His sled felt different when it was towing. Shawn loved the sound of engines, it didn't matter if it was a jet, a hot car or a lawn mower. Amy didn't understand it. She figured it was a guy thing. Only once did she try to understand how it affected Shawn. They were flying to California and Amy noticed Shawn was distracted as the plane approached the runway at their destination. When she asked him what was going on, he said not to bother him as he was listening to the sound of the engines.

Once out on the lake, the fear of sinking subsided quickly and Shawn and Amy simply watched for others traveling in their vicinity. Then Shawn had an idea; he could pinch off the fuel line to the one carburetor and Amy could run up the lake on just one cylinder. It was flat and would be an easy ride. He thought Amy would rather do that than hang off the back of a one-place seat.

So right in the middle of the huge, frozen expanse he coasted to a stop. There was no one else within sight. When Amy got off the sled and stood beside him he told her about his plan. She was uncertain about the fix Shawn had in mind and wasted no time telling Shawn she wasn't crazy about stopping in the middle of "Lake Nowhere" as she now called it.

"Let's just get on with it, Shawn," she said as he lifted the hood of her sled. "I don't like being out here in the middle… Ya know?"

"I know, hun, neither do I, but the ice is supposed to be thicker out here than back there," he pointed toward shore. "I'll be just a minute." He looked for a pair of pliers.

A few seconds later, even before Shawn could get the tool pouch unwrapped, sleds arrived to see if they needed help. Two came from the north and then three showed up from the south. Suddenly there were four more and Shawn wasn't sure where they had come from. They congregated in a circle around Shawn and Amy. Two of the guys got off their sleds and came over to see if there was something they could do. The rest just sat on their idling sleds and waited to see if they would be needed. The accumulated machines sent vibrations through the ice and up through Shawn and Amy's legs.

One of the guys said to Shawn, "If you're towin' up to LacDranna be careful. There's a chasm across the lake on that side… About a foot or so high. If you hit it when it's up, your goin' over, eh!"

Shawn said, "Yeah, yeah, we heard. Thanks. Did somebody drown there today?"

The man said, "Nah, haven't heard about that. Just watch for that crack up there, eh?"

Shawn nodded his appreciation. The pulsating ice made him extremely nervous and he simply closed the hood and waved to all the do-gooders and said, "Thanks. Um, never mind."

He quickly remounted his sled and Amy climbed on behind him. He started the sled and they were off, both of them relieved they weren't sinking to the bottom of the lake. Shawn thought the guys were pretty stupid to park so close together on the ice. He thought they might have known something he didn't but was still concerned that they might have gone in had any more sleds appeared.

They accelerated but it was difficult to see ahead very well. Shawn periodically stood up on the running boards to get a better perspective of the terrain. He was looking for that chasm—if it was even there—and the elevation gave a little better view of the surrounding area.

Each time he did this, Amy tapped him on his thigh. Finally, she pounded him on the leg with her fist. Shawn abruptly let go of the throttle and coasted to a stop. Amy's sled banged against his back bumper.

Shawn climbed off the sled while Amy was still seated and looked her in the eye.

"What the hell's wrong with you now? I'm trying to concentrate, ya know? What's your problem now?"

Amy, in a trembling voice said, "Shawn, if you stand up I'm gonna fall off. I don't have anything to hold onto. It scares me."

Shawn looked behind Amy at the bumper of her sled and realized she was right. He felt really foolish putting Amy in jeopardy like that.

He didn't know what to say so he simply blurted out, "So what do you want me to do? Just hang onto my legs or something...I want to get off of this ice."

Amy just nodded and Shawn got back on feeling even worse. In an attempt to reassure her he reached back and gave her leg a squeeze. He thought she would be okay and for the rest of the tow he remained seated.

As they approached the exit point for the village of LacDranna, Shawn watched for the rift. Ski equipped airplanes were taking people for short rides near where Shawn and Amy needed to exit the lake. The planes were taking off and landing toward Shawn and Amy, and Shawn needed to know their precise flight path. He had difficulty estimating their lift-off point. In addition, he was aware that there could be a slushy spot on the ice.

His tension eased somewhat as the planes passed overhead by a hundred feet or so. He followed their tracks over toward the shore, feeling confident in the integrity of the ice at that point.

There was a lot more activity in the area than when they had ridden onto the ice that morning. Shawn found himself carefully steering his way through small groups of people walking on the lake. Amy thought to herself that it looked like a Currier & Ives painting with a modern twist; kids ice skating on a cleared spot, people pulling little ones on old fashioned "Clipper" sleds, iceboats crossing the lake, and there was a snowmobile club giving short rides to anyone wanting to take them.

As Shawn pulled briskly off the frozen lake and back onto the snow packed beach he looked along the shoreline to where several dozen people stood. They were looking at an odd yellow object protruding out of the water about thirty feet off shore. Shawn stopped the sleds and dismounted, not taking his eyes off of the object. He thought he recognized it as part of a back-hoe excavator. He headed toward the quiet group. The closer he got, the more he was convinced that was what he was seeing. Near the edge of the lake, he stopped and spoke to an older man in a navy P-coat.

Shawn said to the man, "Is that what I think it is? Is that a back-hoe in there?"

"Yes it is," said the man. "They were trying to scrape the ice clear for cutting more block, you know, for the ice castle, and he went in. Right through it; and fast, too." He added, "Ralph's been in before, ice fishing. He'll be ok. I'm sure."

"Oh, good, then," said Shawn. "He'll make it. Some kids told us a guy died up here today after going in."

"Nope, not Ralph. He'll be fine. They took him to Doc. At least one a year goes in and doesn't come out. It's an unknown, that ice."

"Yeah, tell me," Shawn said. "I stopped on a little lake earlier today and found out the water was ten feet below the ice."

"Oh, yeah," said the man. "I heard of one guy that drowned a couple years ago. He actually went over to a waste gate and looked down in—right before he fell through. Pretty dumb I'd say."

"Oh, um, you bet, yeah. How stupid is that, huh?" Shawn said and shook his head.

"How far did you say the water was below the ice today?" the man asked.

Shawn didn't want to appear foolish so he said, "Oh, from the sound of it … you know, probably eight to ten feet. I couldn't tell for sure, you know. You would have to be dumb enough to look down one of those green and yellow cages… ah, waste gates… to be really sure."

"So you were down by the falls today," said the observant man. "That's the only one they painted green and yellow before the weather turned this fall."

"Yeah. The falls weren't much but the lakes were fun to ride on. That is until I found out how little water was below us."

"Well, you have to be careful out there on a snowmobile, and, uh, you would want to stay away from those gates, of course. We really don't need the bad press up here. See ya," said the man as he turned and walked away.

"Oh, ah, thanks for the tip, sir," Shawn said as he turned back to Amy and the sleds.

Shawn said to Amy, "The operator's okay, the kids were wrong. He'll be okay." He then added, "That guy thought I was smart to leave the lake today, down by the falls, ya know? He said someone went in there doin' something stupid a couple years ago… and drowned."

"And what was he doing?"

"Don't know, he's dead, can't ask him now, can we? I'm sure he thought he was doing something safe," Shawn replied knowing where she was going with it.

146

"Or maybe he didn't think at all, huh? You know, sometimes some people don't think at all, right, Shawn?"

Shawn turned away.

"We'll, let's go and see if we can find a dealer to fix your sled. They'll probably be busy, but if I could get the new fuel bowl and gasket I should be able to fix it myself. Drive yours, okay?" Shawn quickly asked without looking back at Amy.

"Oh sure, Shawn," said Amy as she mounted her sled. "Look at all the activity here now. This reminds me of when I was a little kid and my mom took us sledding at Frick Park near Pittsburgh. She would build a fire in an old burn barrel so that I, my sister and our friends could get warm. We used to be out all day and sometimes go back out at night. No wonder I love to do this snowmobiling thing, huh?"

Shawn pointed behind Amy and said, "There's a burn barrel over there. I guess that would have an influence. Yeah, I'm thinking about the first time we ever rode snowmobiles together. When we rented those sleds on our honeymoon at Six Springs Ski Resort. Remember? They made us all go real slow, single file for an hour, like those free rides over there," he pointed to where the snowmobile club was taking on passengers.

"Boy, now that seems boring." Amy replied. "Of course, back then, to us it was just a blast. And then remember they closed the whole ski place to sleds 'cause that one lady wrecked and she wasn't wearing a helmet and was still in a coma when she arrived back where she lived in Denver. Remember that?"

"Yeah, I guess the insurance premiums killed them. I think they're doing it again, there, now though. Thought I read that in the paper somewhere."

"How about you, Shawn? Did you go out a lot on regular sleds when you were a kid?"

"All of the time, Amy. Yeah, me and my brother. We'd get our dad to pull us along the county road, the original two-up sled. Then when he would get tired and go back home, we'd ride down Reis Run Road. That one by the old house that was really steep. That is, if they didn't plow it and the traffic was light. A couple of times we tried to help push some cars up it, but of course they'd never make it. Then we'd have to dodge them on the way back down. One time my brother ran right under the running board of one of those big old 4X4 trucks. He was okay, but cut his forehead a little. We had to pry him out. I'm thinking those regular, old fashioned sleds were more dangerous than what we're on now, huh?"

"I would say so; no brakes," Amy said as she put her helmet back on. "I think all kids ought to wear helmets now, though. Especially on regular sleds. I know I could have used one a couple times."

"Amy, tell me it's not true. You never wrecked your sled when you were little, did you?"

"Well, since you had to ask, yup."

"No!"

"Well, and I don't want this repeated, they called me 'Slow Steer Amy' in my neighborhood. But just for a while, though," she added quickly.

"Get out!" Shawn said with a smile on his face. "Come to think of it, I guess I can believe that. What did you do to earn that one?"

"A couple of things, I guess. One, I wasn't strong enough to steer quickly so I was all over the place with my sled. The funny one that comes to mind, though, was the time we were riding on Highland golf course and some kid that lived down the block, Ray, he passed me up and cut me off going down the hill. I got him at the bottom, though," Amy said proudly.

"What do you mean you 'got him at the bottom'?"

"Well, I ran over him after he hit a little pipe or something sticking out of the ground. Yup, he stopped fast and I ran right up and over his butt." Amy said proudly.

"You're kidding. On purpose?"

"Well, duh, yeah. He had it coming."

"Did he get hurt?"

"A little. They said he had these little chunks of skin taken out of each vertebra up his back from the front edge of my sled. It was funny, he was screaming and crying with me sitting on top of him. Big baby, I think he still liked me, though, 'cause he asked me to go to our senior dance in high school, years after that."

"Did you go?"

"Hell no. He probably wanted to get me back or something."

"Did you get into trouble?"

"Nope. 'Cause I told my mom and dad about a pass and I kind of insinuated that he... well, they thought I meant that he made a *pass*. You know? So they called up his house and yelled at his parents. He got into more trouble then, I think, but anyway, that was one of 'em," said Amy with the smile Shawn adored.

"Ruthless… And shameless. I'll know better than to pass you again on these sleds," as he walked back to his snowmobile.

Before he twisted the key, he pushed his face shield back up and turned to Amy and yelled, "And stay off my butt."

Passersby heard his remark and glanced at Amy as if she could not handle her snowmobile while it was being towed. Amy just nodded and smiled back at Shawn knowing there was no need to explain it to anyone.

They wound their way through the crowd in the lakeside park and stopped by the gazebo to ask several people for directions to the repair shop.

After waiting for an hour just to get to speak with a mechanic, Shawn got the bad news. No "fix" parts available, and a new replacement carburetor, installed, would cost them $500. Shawn didn't like spending the money but knew the chances of fixing it on his own were slim. The mechanic could get the job done in several hours so he reluctantly gave the go ahead.

Shawn and Amy doubled up on his sled and rode the mile or so back to their hotel room to unwind from the days ride. If the sled ran well enough when it was done they might do a night ride, just around the village trails, after dinner.

They got back to their room about four o'clock. The maid had left the door wide open and they noticed another "gift" on the pillow of the perfectly made-up bed. Amy thought she would not have been so abrupt with the woman that morning if she had gotten a good night's sleep in a warm bed. Maybe tomorrow she would thank the maid, but she would go the rest of the day without a thank you, even if she saw her. Amy held grudges for at least a day or two, sometimes longer. But never less than a day.

Shawn closed the door to the connecting room, and propped the ladder back chair under the door knob. Although they were both coming to grips with their newly imposed room situation, it still felt like all their belongings were out there and could be searched, inspected or sorted through. It was not a comfortable feeling for a couple who paid over two thousand dollars and a high monthly fee for their home security system.

Amy said as Shawn closed the bathroom door, "Another reason *not* to have a gun up here. Someone would have had that by now, I'll bet."

Shawn, taking off his snowmobile suit, answered without looking at Amy, "I would have had it with me. That's why I would have it here, to take on the trails *with* me. Get it, Amy?"

"Yeah, I do, but see, hun, today was no problem at all. Besides, you might have shot yourself during your Xtreme riding demo," she laughed.

"Oh, funny," replied Shawn, as he climbed onto the bedspread in his life saving, long johns. "I'm napping for a while. Get me up when you want to do dinner. Okay?"

"And who's gonna wake me up?" sliding onto the bed from the other side.

"No hurry I guess, then. We'll eat whenever we get up."

Thinking with his eyes closed for a few seconds, he added, "Oh, oh, what time did we have reservations for? Seven? Seven thirty?"

"Yeah, I think so. I guess I'll set the clock for six or so."

A short while after they dozed off, they were awakened by a soft tapping and a call from the hallway.

"Mister Kaan, the sled is here. I have your sled here. Mr. Kaan?"

Shawn sat up and said, "Huh?"

He was disoriented and thought he must be dreaming. Was it like the time, years ago, when Amy made the hour and a half "surprise" trip to visit him in the late evening while he was in college? He was trying to clear his head then, too.

Shawn had gone hunting after classes during the early afternoon hours and had come back to his off-campus, second floor room, worn out and without any game to show for his effort. Amy had called his landlady about 8:00 PM, while he was napping, and been told that Shawn must have gone back to the college library to do research.

Amy, at that time being a little less than secure in her relationship with Shawn, talked a friend into going with her to Shawn's' boarding house to see if, in fact, he was out late working or into some other kind of activity. By the time she arrived at the large mansion-turned-private-dorm, it was close to 11:00 PM and all the lights in the house were out. Shawn was sound asleep in his cozy corner room.

Just as now, Shawn awakened to tapping noises and a voice calling his name. Groggy and not realizing yet where he was or what time of day or night it was, he listened for a few minutes, trying to clear his head. He thought his landlady may have been right; that her older, deceased sister *did* come back to 'visit,' rising out of the water well that was just below Shawn's window.

By the time he got up out of bed he could hear a couple of female voices below his room. They were giggling and talking and throwing bits of gravel at his window.

More awake now, he knew who it was. Some local high school kids had recently been having sex under the shrubs, right outside that corner of the house while waiting for their bus. Shawn and the other boarders knew this because they had found a used condom a few days before. The resident college students told their landlady they'd watch and try to find out who the perpetrators were; maybe even catch them in the 'act.'

Shawn, upset at the thought that they would now be harassing him, threw open the window and, standing there in his BVD's, yelled, "Get outta here you little assholes!"

His voice ricocheted through the neighborhood. There was nothing but an eerie quiet for several seconds.

Then he heard a sheepish voice coming from the darkness below, "Shawn, it's me, Amy. It's Amy, Shawn."

Amy and her friend, Kay, met him at the kitchen door and they all had a good laugh about it. They talked in the kitchen for about half an hour and then the girls left for the long trip home. Amy didn't say much about it to Shawn, but Kay hinted to him later that Amy thought he might have been out partying with someone else that night and he had made it home just before she arrived. Shawn gave her the actual timeline but there was no way to really prove he was telling the truth… that is until eight years later.

As Shawn was throwing out some of the old letters Amy had sent to him in college, he found the proof he actually needed long ago. It was a paper that was tucked between two, yellowing love letters. He couldn't remember, but he must have been keeping it in support of his alibi to Amy.

It was a short note to Shawn from his landlady. She had apologized to Amy through Shawn. The landlady didn't know that Shawn had been in his room all evening when Amy called on the phone. She wanted Shawn to tell Amy she was sorry for the misinformation. 'Ol' Huddsie,' as she was affectionately called, since she drove an antique Hudson car, was like that, never one to step on any toes.

When he showed Amy the new found evidence, she just laughed about it being so long after the fact. Although it wasn't a big deal now, to Shawn it was just a little something that he had wished he could set straight with her. He believed little things like that added up over time, and could either strengthen or weaken a relationship. He felt vindicated; she thought it was funny he even cared.

This time, of course, it wasn't Amy's voice and again someone called out, "Mr. Kaan, I have your sled for you. It's done."

"Oh, ah, yeah, be right there," Shawn replied.

Amy stirred and said in a whisper, "The checkbook's over there in my suit case, hun."

Shawn got up from the bed and, sorting through the suit case Amy pointed at, he finally found the blue checkbook. Still in his long johns, he picked up a pen on the nightstand and walked through the bathroom and opened their hallway door wider. A man in greasy coveralls stood in front of him with the key and some paperwork in his blackened hands.

Shawn said yawning, "How ya doing? Get it fixed, huh?"

"Yep, sure did, and found some parts, so Tom said it was only $39.00, ah, U.S., please."

"Great! It's okay, though, huh? It'll work like it used to, right?" as he wrote out the check.

"Oh sure, yep, good as new," he took the check and wrote down the check number on the receipt, which he then handed to Shawn along with the key.

"Wow, thanks…Wait here a minute," he turned quickly and ducked back into the room.

Shawn grabbed a ten dollar bill off the dresser by the window and went back toward the door.

Amy said, "What's up? Did I hear forty bucks?"

"Yep, lucked out… saved some money this time."

He tried to give the waiting mechanic the ten dollars but it was refused.

"No, really, here ya go," Shawn said, "Have a drink or some lunch," he handed the money toward the man again.

"Oh, no, thanks. Normally I would but Tom said not to. Have a good ride," as he turned toward the stairs.

"Well, okay. Hey, does Tom happen to run a groomer? Am I thinking that's the same Tom?"

"Day and night," came the reply from the man. "Not sure how he does it, but yeah, that'd be him. Good guy, old Tom. Oh, and he said to tell you he threw the trail sticker on there for ya, too. The other ones in your hand there," pointing at the receipt Shawn was holding.

"Wow, thank him for me, okay?"

"Sure 'nough," said the mechanic and, reaching the stairway, bounded down as if he was now late.

Shawn re-entered the bath and then the bedroom as Amy sat up in bed.

Shawn said, "Can you believe it? Tom, the groomer guy, owns that shop, I guess. Fixed the sled cheap and gave us our trail permits. You know, stickers… Free."

"Great," said Amy, "Boy, a little help goes a long way around here, huh? Kinda like the 'payin' it forward' thing in the movie.

"Yeah. So far some nice people up here. And I hardly did anything."

"It's about five-thirty," said Amy, "Why don't we see if we can go down to dinner early and then take a short ride around town here? What do you think?"

"Yeah, I'd be up for that. Then we could put more miles on tomorrow. I'd like you to make sure it's running good before taking another long ride."

They got dressed and simply walked out of the room, not even attempting to close the hallway door. They were feeling a little more comfortable with the arrangement. They cast a quick glance toward the open doorway of their, as yet unseen, neighbor.

A Night To Remember

When they entered the dining room area they were impressed. For an out of the way village in Canada, the atmosphere was decidedly up-scale and "citified." The maitre de' met them at the entrance and seemed to know their names.

"Kaan? Ah, early, but that's fine," she said with a smile. "Right this way please," turning toward the left side of the restaurant. She arrived at a nicely appointed table for four near a large picture window and placed their menus down carefully.

"Have an enjoyable meal," she said as she cleared the two extra place settings and turned back toward the entrance.

Shawn thanked her and they took their seats. Amy looked through the slightly frosted window and said to Shawn, "Check *that* out."

The complete shore line of the lake was lighted with red road flares, spaced about a hundred feet apart and it seemed to go on for miles in both directions. Outside, just between the restaurant and the lake, was a large ice castle illuminated with multi-colored floodlights. There was a yellow flaming torch attached to a dragon's mouth on top of it. The ice castle was approximately twenty feet tall, twenty feet deep and forty to fifty feet long. The colored lights seemed to be within the walls of the castle and they could see where the joints had been made between the huge hand cut blocks of ice from the lake. The thick middle parts were as clear as glass and the joints were opaque silver. All around the castle were life size ice carvings of horses, pelicans, bears and snowmobiles. People milled in and out.

"Wow," said Shawn, "Just like Chautauqua Lake. How did we miss that this morning? Neat."

Just then the waiter arrived with, "Spectacular, eh? My name is Justin. Can I get you some water?"

Amy and Shawn simultaneously said, "Yes, please," and turned back to the window.

Shawn said to the waiter, "Very nice. We've gone to a place in New York, Chautauqua Lake, which has an ice castle like that every year. Not quite as big, but close."

"Yeah, but we never expected to see one right outside our window here. Really nice," Amy added. "We'll go down there—maybe later, Shawn? What a neat place, huh?"

The waiter added, "It'll be on until midnight through Sunday night. It helps us out here, I know. Here are our specials tonight. I'll be right back with your water."

Shawn ordered an end cut prime rib and Amy her favorite, a lobster tail.

As they enjoyed their excellently prepared meal and sipped some wine they talked about returning to the area some day.

"I wonder if we'll ever get back here again. Maybe with some friends next time," Shawn said.

"Yeah, I sometimes think about all the neat places we've been to—but only once, and we never seem to be able to get back," said Amy. "I guess if we'd make an effort to re-run our paths sometimes, it would be interesting. Maybe in retirement, huh?"

"I guess so," said Shawn. "Although I just remembered, I recommended eating at that crab place near Santa Monica pier to my friend at work a few years ago when he went to California. Like we did before catching our flight home, remember?"

Amy smiled and nodded her head.

"Ya know, he was still pissed when I saw him a month after returning," Shawn said. "According to him, he, his wife and their little son were absolutely deluged with street people and beggars all around that area when they came out of the restaurant. He said he feared for their safety. And he's a really big, well-built guy." Shawn continued, "I mean, I didn't know. It was only five years or so since we were there and it was great then. I think we would have to check each place out before going back. Things change sometimes and you might never know it or expect it to be totally different."

"Maybe that old saying about 'You can never go home again,' applies to things like traveling together, too," Amy said and then paused. She quietly added "So... maybe we make a little vow tonight, you and me, bucco, to start enjoying each step of our lives more as we go through them—together—just the two of us...'Cause we never know if we'll make it back or not," she raised her wine glass in a toast.

"Sounds good to me," said Shawn and looked Amy in the eyes. He lifted his glass. He thought briefly about the name incident and then dismissed it as Amy had requested. "This trip could prove to be a turning point in our lives together. Maybe we needed a fresh start, huh? What do you think, Amy? We need a new start?"

Amy realized Shawn knew something had changed since he was gone. She knew he suspected there was

159

someone else in the picture. She said softly, "Sure, why not?" and clinked her glass against Shawn's.

They both smiled a little and then turned back toward the activity outside their window, staring quietly and hoping they really would have a long, memorable life together.

When the dessert menu arrived they were too full to sample anything; they both declined.

Amy said, "It's pushing seven. Wanna get ready and ride a little before bed?"

"Sure, go ahead and get suited up. I'll take care of the bill and be right up," Shawn replied.

"Sounds good," said Amy. "Let's make it a short one, though, I think it's getting cold out."

Just then their waiter came with the check and as Amy left, Shawn handed him his credit card.

"Oh, you can put this on the room tab if you'd like, sir," the waiter said.

"Okay, good."

He signed his name and added their room number to the bill.

"Your tip," picking up the twenty dollar bill from under the sugar bowl and handing it to the waiter. He added, "It was great, thanks."

"No, thank *you,* sir," came the reply and he smiled adding, "And please come back soon."

"Oh, I think we will."

As he reached the front of the inn, Shawn wondered where the mechanic had left Amy's sled. He had to pick his way through a large group of men waiting to get into the bar that was overflowing into the wide hallway. None of them were wearing snowmobile garb so he assumed they must be locals. When he turned and looked out the front window he overheard a couple of men laughing and talking quietly about something that apparently had just happened.

One rough looking, forty-something guy, who actually looked kind of familiar to Shawn, said to the younger skinny one, "Don't worry about it. She didn't slap you, did she? Just me. 'Course all you grabbed was a little ass. Felt good to me, though. Nice 'n warm down there." Both of them laughed out loud.

Shawn saw Amy's sled just in front of the entry steps then turned his attention back to the conversation he had just heard. Who were these creeps talking about? There were no women present and none outside that he could see. *Could they be talking about Amy?* he wondered. *She did just pass through here.* As he excused himself and pushed through the crowd toward the steps, he came eye to eye for a second with the burly guy. The guy tipped his head just a bit as if trying to place Shawn's face. Shawn quickly looked away and continued to the steps and started to climb them.

As he did, he heard some snickering behind him and a different voice, the young skinny guy, saying loud enough for Shawn to hear, "He's a lucky 'sombitch, eh?"

There was a bit of laughing and grumbling as Shawn wound his way up the steps.

When he reached the room he found the door closed tightly. Apparently the chair was up against it as it banged loudly when he tried to open it.

Amy said, "Shawn?"

"Yeah, it's me. Open up."

161

Amy did and grabbing Shawn by the arm pulled him inside. She closed the door with a bang.

"Where the hell were you, Shawn?" she shouted at him. "Those bastards just groped me! Downstairs in the lobby, they grabbed me, Shawn. Where *were* you?"

Shawn defended himself by saying, "I was taking care of the bill, remember? I heard them joking about a girl. It was you, then?"

"Yeah. Those bastards." Amy said, her voice quivering, "What are you gonna do, Shawn? You gotta do *something*. I can't let them get away with that shit, no way, Shawn."

"Well what did you do? What did you say to them?"

"What the hell does *that* mean, Shawn? What do you mean 'What did *I* do?' Are you suggesting I said or did something to warrant this? Is that what you're saying, Shawn? What? I called them the wrong name? You're blaming me for this?"

"No, I guess not, I mean I don't understand why they would just attack you in the open like that, that's all."

"'Cause they did, Shawn. They *did*." Amy started to cry.

"I don't know, Amy. Just lookin' at them ...They really seemed like bad news. You'd have to come back for court or something if you pressed charges. And who would be a witness? They would all lie for each other."

Amy said pleadingly, "You mean you're gonna let this go? Some pig sticks his hand down my pants and you want to let it go? I don't believe you don't have the guts, Shawn."

"Well, give me a minute to think, hun. I'll do something, Amy, but you need to think about where we are right now. We're not in the U.S. You'll never get a fair shake up here. Think about the fight we saw the other night. I'll bet that's a way of life up here."

"Oh, shit, Amy. I just realized where I saw that guy that groped you before. It's him! The big guy that beat up the little guy…You know, back in the village. Now I know why his eyes looked familiar. I… I don't know, Amy. The guy is obviously a nut case. He's probably just out of jail or headed back there or something. He's bad news, I'll bet."

"You think that's him? Or you're *sure* that's him, Shawn?" Amy said as she slowly sank onto the toilet seat lid," I guess I can agree to let it slide if we'd be in real danger." She added, "But you need to be sure it's him, okay? If it isn't that wacko, I'm gonna burn his ass. Got it? So find out if it's him, Shawn."

"How the hell am I supposed to do that?"

"I don't know, but I'll call the cops if it's not that wacko."

"Okay… okay. I'll go down and ask somebody something… Be right back," he gave Amy a hug. "Block the door."

"I'm going to take a shower. I feel dirty."

"It's probably not your fault, Amy. He's a pig. Like you said…maybe he does it all the time. Somebody should break his hand." Shawn said.

"Probably? Probably? Nice, Shawn. Just go away. Get away from me."

"I'm sorry, Amy. I'm pissed, too. I'm not thinking straight here, okay?"

"And don't try to do something physical yourself, Shawn," Amy whispered. "I'm okay. It's not worth you getting hurt over... I'm just so pissed about it. But I don't want you to do anything violent, okay? You know, too, you don't want to give the Army any reason to screw you any more than they have."

"Okay, hun," Shawn said, giving her a kiss on the cheek, that instantly was turned away. "I'll just try to find out if it's him. The Army? I'd like to have just one thing from them right now; my old weapon."

As he passed by the bar area he could hear loud laughter from the group that molested Amy. He had a thought and walked briskly to the restaurant. There was no one at the reservation desk, so he waited.

When the receptionist arrived, he asked to speak to Justin, their waiter from earlier, and she went to get him.

Shawn pulled him aside and quietly asked if he would go through the bar and see if he could recognize the person Shawn described. Justin agreed and made a pass through the area where the group was drinking heavily. He nodded as he returned to Shawn a minute or so later.

"The big one in the dirty white coveralls, over in the corner, is Bruno. The other, skinny one they call 'Snowman.' Bruno, the big guy, is real bad news. He and his brother are from the states. They're always in trouble around here. What'd he do this time?" the waiter asked.

Shawn said," Oh, he grabbed my wife, out there," he pointed over his shoulder. "Would you know if he was in a bad fight down the road the other night?"

164

"I don't know but I wouldn't doubt it. If you give me a little time I can find out, eh?" the waiter said.

"Okay, I'd appreciate that. Thanks," Shawn said as he extended a five dollar bill.

"No...That's okay, sir," was the waiter's response.

Shawn said, "Well, okay. I gotta say, most of the people we met around here are really great. But some ... Wow."

"Well, they're not from here, remember? They're from the states, eh?" the waiter added with a smile. "They're just a bad influence on some of our locals. If you had witnesses and pressed charges—*and* could make them stick—they might get expelled from the country. For some reason, they never seem to serve time for the stuff they do. They must know someone. Not sure what they did back in the states but I know they throw a lot of money around up here."

"Yeah, I thought about charges but we don't have any witnesses," Shawn stated. "I think it'd be futile at this point. But thanks, and let me know if it was this guy or his brother in that fight the other night, alright?"

"Will do," said the waiter. "And good luck. Remember, he's a bad one and has a lot of nasty friends. Be *very* careful."

"I will."

Shawn looked away from the bar area as he passed the doorway and returned to their room.

"Amy? Amy?" Shawn said tapping at the door.

"Yeah... okay, Shawn."

She was wrapped in a towel and still wet, but Shawn hugged her anyway.

165

"The waiter is gonna find out if it's him or not. Could have been his brother in that fight. But in any case, he said they're really bad news. From our country, rich with a lot of friends up here. He said to be very careful around him."

"Great, just great. Couldn't be just a regular pig, had to be a dangerous, rich one, huh?"

"We'll see, Amy. Maybe we can get some local help. That Tom guy seems to be pretty influential around here. Maybe I'll ask him if it's worth pursuing."

"I guess. But I'm not a happy camper, Shawn."

"I know, I know, hun, me neither. But if it's gonna go nowhere, why tell 'em who we are. You know, in court he'd find out all about us. He's from the states, remember?" Shawn said as he again gave her a reassuring hug.

"Yeah, I guess. Why do guys do things like that, Shawn?"

"Don't know, babe. I guess 'cause he'd never be able to do it with permission. Twisted world nowadays. I know what I'd do to him in Iraq."

"I'm not going out to ride tonight, not now, and I'm sleeping in my suit. That door is staying shut tight. I don't care about the heat. Got it, Shawn? I don't want you to open that door at all tonight," Amy declared.

"You got it, hun, and again, I'll see what Tom thinks tomorrow."

"Okay. And I'll try not to let it ruin the rest of our vacation."

She pulled on her long johns and then her snowmobile suit and quietly crawled into bed.

"Good, babe," Shawn whispered. Let's go to sleep early and ride early, okay? New day tomorrow, right?"

"Alright," as she kissed him. "I'm really lucky. You're so unlike most guys. I love you."

"Love you, too, for always, Amy," Shawn said and he held her until she fell asleep. He hoped she wouldn't waken until morning.

He thought about the wonderful, adventurous day of riding they had had and hoped the bad incident wouldn't make Amy decide she wanted to go home early. Then he did what he was prone to do, started on a guilt trip, second guessing himself about what he could have done differently so Amy wouldn't have had to go through that ordeal. He thought about what it would be like to be really big and strong or well armed enough to preserve his wife's honor. He began to feel like a wimp, and woke up numerous times during the night, breathing hard, dreaming about being in a fight with the bad guy. He hated it. He wanted to be able to take his gun and go downstairs in front of the guy's buddies, blast him in the hand, and then go calmly back to bed—just like Dirty Harry would. But he couldn't, so he tossed and turned and struggled to get some sleep.

All too soon, the room began to lighten. Shawn didn't think he had gotten any sleep but, all told, he had gotten a couple of hours. Amy had tossed and turned, too.

Shawn got up to take his shower. As he recalled the incidents of the night before, he felt bad for Amy. He hoped this wouldn't be long lived; he had heard stories about women that had been assaulted or raped, then not wanting to have anything to do with their husband, a victim as well. He thought she would probably be okay after they returned home, but decided not to touch her in any way she might deem sexual, just in case. As he dried off, he heard Amy stretching and yawning as usual, making her funny, whimpering sounds.

"Amy? Amy? How'd ya sleep, hun?" he asked through the door.

"Fair, I guess," Came her answer. "I gotta go. Almost done in there?"

"Yeah, " he said as he opened the door. They kissed and traded places.

"I'll be in to brush my teeth in a sec," Shawn said.

"No, can't. Gotta go, gotta go," Amy responded.

"Well, I'll get dressed first, then," said Shawn. "Do you think you want to ride for awhile, and then eat? Or eat around here and ride later?"

Amy hesitated and then talked through the bathroom door. She said, "Definitely not around here. I'm not eating around here today. Figure it out. We'll eat in some other town. Let's ride first."

"No problem, just wanted to know if I should get dressed for riding." Shawn said.

Amy didn't reply, so Shawn went about getting his snowmobile suit on. Amy's was in a pile at the foot of the bed and Shawn wasn't sure if she took it off in the middle of the night or when she got out of bed.

By the time he was dressed, standing in his bib's and holding his jacket, he heard a flush and Amy came out of the bathroom. She had a serious look on her face and Shawn knew that meant trouble.

She said,"And I want something done about that creep. I can't let him get away with that. I want him punished somehow. I've decided. I don't care if he *is* crazy."

Shawn immediately went to her side and gave her a hug.

"I know, Amy, I want to get him for that, too. Like I said, I'll talk to Tom and see how well he knows the local JP or whatever they have up here," Shawn answered.

"Well, we better do it early. What if he leaves the area?" She asked as she put on her thermal socks.

"Okay, early it is, Amy," Shawn said.

Second Day's Ride

Amy knew the groper wasn't staying at the inn, but just walking by the area where he had touched her made her nervous. She hurried through the foyer and skipped down the steps to her waiting snowmobile. Shawn put the key in the ignition for her and gave it a twist. Unlike the last time she tried, the engine fired immediately and they grinned at each other. They had something to smile about again.

Shawn walked around the side of the building and with a quick pull, started his snowmobile easily as well. He thought they may want to ride another direction entirely today; maybe change the whole paradigm for a time. Then he remembered a spectacular trail Jay had told him about—almost insisting he ride there. He mounted his sled and turned around to join Amy waiting to leave the lot.

"We'll need fuel. Might as well save the cans and get it here before heading out, huh?" he said to Amy.

She nodded and Shawn took the lead. He pulled out of the lot onto the snow-packed street, waiting until after some other sleds went by. The convenience store/ gas station where he bought coffee yesterday morning was the closest. He would have preferred a more modern facility so as not to get watered fuel, but he pulled in beside the pumps anyway and edged forward so he could fill both sleds from the same nozzle. He didn't pay attention to the cost because for now, anyway, money was not the problem.

After he filled the tanks he went inside and gave the attendant fifty dollars. Shawn held out his hand for the change. The attendant counted out the amount with a southern drawl. Shawn remembered the same accent from the creep that had said Shawn was lucky last night. Shawn figured it was possibly the same person. He could hardly keep from saying something, but he knew it would be better not to tip him off about how upset they were. If the big guy knew they were looking for him he may make himself scarce until Shawn and Amy were gone from the area.

The attendant seemed really nice and Shawn started to doubt it was the same guy after all. To Shawn, all southern accents sounded alike so maybe he was wrong. Then, just as he opened the door, the attendant said, "You're a lucky sombitch today. Ridin' is great out there!"

Shawn spun around. He had all he could do not to jump the counter and punch the guy as hard as he could. He now knew his was the voice from the night before. He walked back to the counter and stretched out his hand with five dollars in it. The attendant smiled and reached for the money. Shawn grabbed two of the guy's fingers and, looking the attendant in the eyes, he slowly bent them both back until he heard a loud pop. The attendant screamed and fell on the counter swearing. He grabbed his fingers. Shawn stared at him for perhaps five seconds then turned and pushed through the door.

The attendant started to flail his arms and was yelling that he was going to kill Shawn.

Shawn expected him to come storming out after him, but he didn't have the guts. He stood on the other side of the window, cradling his hand and yelling.

"What's wrong with *him*, Shawn? Look at him. How'd ya set him off like that?"

"Guess he wanted a tip," Shawn said and shrugged as he started his engine.

As they pulled away from the pumps the attendant seemed to realize who they were. Shawn saw him look at Amy and then look across the street to the inn. Shawn didn't much care if he knew who they were now.

They re-crossed the street and took the trail that they used from Tom's shop the day before. It was only about a mile away and they got there quickly. The parking lot was full of sleds and Shawn doubted they would be able to talk to Tom this time of the day. He dismounted and walked to Amy.

Shawn said, "It looks like he's really busy, Amy. I probably won't be able to talk to him right now."

"You promised, Shawn."

"Well, alright, okay, I'll try then," Shawn said and turned toward the front door with a blinking sign saying 'Open.'

As soon as Shawn entered the shop he knew it would be impossible to have a private conversation with Tom. There were at least eight other people waiting to get service and he didn't feel right about talking to Tom—or anyone—about what had happened the night before, in public.

As he turned to leave he heard a woman at the counter say to someone that Tom was still out grooming trails and might not be in at all today.

Shawn told Amy what he had heard and she was willing to wait a little longer but not until tomorrow. Shawn would need to get something going later today, *or else*. She didn't say what the 'or else' was, but Shawn thought he knew what it would be; Amy would want to pack up and leave for home as soon as they got back from today's ride. He meant to try to talk to someone by nightfall so she would know he was being supportive.

A man wearing wire rimmed glasses, at least six feet tall and looking to be in his late fifties, walked up to the snowmobile parked next to Shawn's just as he sat down.

"Hey, nice snowmobile. Are you two from around here?" he asked.

Shawn considered all that had happened recently and hesitated just long enough to size the guy up while he put his gloves on.

"No, no, we're not. Why?"

"Well, are you riding somewhere special today? 'Cause if you're not, my wife Karla and I, would appreciate the company. We're thinking about going up to the local club's cook-out at noon. Up at, ah, um, wellhead number twenty-six, up there," he turned and pointed to the open spot near the top of one of the mountains.

Shawn had been down that road before and just glanced at the spot for a few seconds.

"I don't know. How far is it?"

"Oh, about thirty or forty miles, I guess," said the man. "Never been there, but I heard it's really neat. We're a little nervous about going alone. We've never been up here before. We usually ride in New York."

"Oh yeah? " Shawn replied, warming up to the conversation. "What part of New York? We ride there too."

"Just outside of Rome, toward Tug Hill. We usually stay around there, or maybe Old Forge; that's pretty. But we had a couple extra days this week and thought we would take a ride in a different place, you know, see if we like it." The man added, "We do...like it, I mean. But it's a little more rugged up here than we're used to. I don't want to get lost up there."

Shawn looked at Amy and she shrugged okay.

Shawn said, "Sure. Guess we could go along. Do we have to register or something?"

"No, I read in the shop here, you just show up. I guess it's $5.00 a head. I'm Dean, by the way. That's my wife, Karla," he pointed at the woman on a blue sled that matched his in color.

"Shawn," he said and then nodded at Amy, "My wife, Amy. We're from Pennsylvania."

Shawn stared at the front of Dean's suit.

"I wouldn't think you *could* get lost with all that." He pointed to a portable G.P.S. unit that dangled from Dean's neck; a compass behind it; ear plugs leading to something electronic strapped on the sled and a cell phone poking out of his front top pocket.

"Oh, this stuff?" said Dean as he moved it around like he was aiming it at a satellite. "Yeah, always have it along," he said with a grin. "But, you know, my phone doesn't always work away from New York, it's my work cell."

"What about that?" Shawn said as he pointed toward two 6-inch black antennas attached to the cowling of Dean's hood. "What are they for?"

174

"Oh, um, it's nothing. Well, ah, old mobile phone things. You know, land line phone stuff. Just didn't take them off yet."

"Almost looks military," said Shawn as he reached toward one of the antennas.

Dean slowly and deliberately blocked Shawn's hand.

"Old. Kind of fragile, um, but couldn't be military. Got them at Radio Shack. Of course, on second thought, maybe they could be military after all." They all laughed.

Shawn said, "No, I'm... well, I *was* in the military and we used ones just like those in Iraq. Powerful little suckers! Super range. *Nothing* stops the signal. I just didn't know they were available state side."

"I guess all that stuff comes back sooner or later," then quickly changing the subject, Dean said, "Hey, I don't know about you two but we haven't eaten any breakfast, so if you'd go with us I'd like to get on up there. What do you think?"

Karla, ready to put on her helmet stopped long enough to add, "Dean's been a Boy Scout since he was fifteen. He's got everything with him that he'd ever need to stay out here for weeks," she laughed. "Yeah, if it's electronic, and Wal-Mart or Radio Shack sells it, he's got it!"

Shawn had a flash-back to Chuck Wagon carrying his house with him and he glanced toward Amy. She nodded a little and smiled. He knew she was thinking it, too.

"Well good, then," Shawn said. "If I break down I'll know who to call."

Dean smiled and mounted his sled. He looked at Shawn and pointed to a map on his tank.

"I can get us close."

Shawn fired up his sled and waved.

Dean led, then Karla, followed by Amy then Shawn. They picked up a trail heading east toward the mountainous terrain. A short distance from town they found they were in the outback, thick with waist high shrubbery and old growth pine trees and large maples.

The trail had begun narrow, only wide enough for one sled but soon opened up and merged with a wide logging road. The roadway was different than any Shawn had ever seen. It made a series of left and right banked, sweeping turns; probably twenty of them, equally spaced and going on for some miles. They were able to speed along at 55 miles per hour, the province's top legal speed and passed several sleds headed in the opposite direction.

They quickly covered 20 miles and Dean stopped at an intersection in the woods. He turned to Shawn who was still riding in the rear and motioned for him to come to the front. They all dismounted for a stretch.

Shawn was impressed with Dean's over-the-counter type of GPS. It clearly showed the intersection with coordinates and trails leading out. A blue x was blinking. There was even a large deer feeding corn crib that showed up across the intersection.

Dean said, "That's us, here," he pointed to the blinking blue x. "It's within three feet of where we actually are. I'm thinking about another 20 miles and we're there. I put the club's trails on it at home before we left."

"That's neat, Dean. But it can't be within three feet. That's the military GPS version. The civilian one is only to within 15 feet. Trust me, I know! They might have told you that to sell you but it can't be that close." Shawn said emphatically, "Regular people can't get the mil spec one, guaranteed!"

Dean looked puzzled and hesitated before he said, "Oh, ah, yep, you're absolutely right, Shawn. I forgot. That *is* what they said at Wal-Mart…er…ah, Radio Shack. It's within 15 feet, yes, 15. That's right. It's the military that is 3 feet. Yep, you are correct, sir. Sorry, didn't mean to exaggerate there. Heh, heh."

Shawn was really impressed now. He looked at Amy and pointed at the GPS, then to himself and said, "Birthday, uh huh."

She wasn't aware of what he was looking at on the screen, but did hear the word "birthday" clearly. She nodded as if she knew what he wanted.

They all remounted and made a right turn and whisked off down a smooth, wide roadway. Shawn realized Dean and Karla hadn't ridden a lot, because they slowed for bends a lot more than he and Amy, but they made up for it on the straight-aways They were going close to 50 miles per hour in spots so he wasn't complaining.

Soon, Dean slowed and turned right onto another trail. It meandered deeper into the forest and then opened up suddenly onto a three or four acre flat spot. The access road split and they took the one to the right, passing a roped off wellhead. When they approached the edge of the mountain, they saw there were about a hundred snowmobiles parked randomly. People stood around one snowmobile with a long trailer attached. On the trailer there was a commercial-sized gas grill. Pots steamed and a man turned hot dogs and hamburgers. There was a long line waiting for food.

As soon as Amy dismounted she said, "If we want anything I think we better get in line right away."

Shawn took his key out of his sled said, "Good idea. Check out the view, though," he pointed over the edge.

They all oohed and awed and then headed for the food line.

Shawn said, "Kind'a like looking down at Markus' place the other day, huh Amy?"

"Yeah, it does. Way up here like this."

Dean overheard him and asked, "Did you say Markus, Shawn?"

Shawn said, "Oh, yeah. We met some guy the other day at a game dinner, on our way up here. Guess he's a big fish in a little pond in upstate New York. Had a neat camp and all. Looked like this. The view from the mountain above it, that is."

"Ah, near Fort Drum, was it?" mumbled Dean.

"No, middle of nowhere," Shawn laughed. "Actually, just outside the Adirondack Forest Preserve, northwest of it. Know him?"

"Hmm, Fort Drum. Ah, no, never met him. Heard about him," Dean replied.

"Guess it would be pretty close to Fort Drum, come to think about it," said Shawn.

"Interesting," said Dean, deep in thought. "So it's Fort Drum." He then quickly added, "I'm really hungry now. How 'bout you, Shawn?"

"About the same as before; yeah, hungry," he said.

They took their place in line and as they were standing there, a young boy came by to collect money for the lunch. They heard a bull horn say no beer was allowed, and to please give them time to be sure the food was thoroughly cooked. They were also assured there would be plenty of food to go around, so no one should leave early or hungry.

Dean, Karla, Shawn and Amy made small talk while they waited their turn in line. They talked about their sleds and how long they had been riding, where they started and how they wound up here. They figured they wouldn't stay in touch but it was interesting and a way to pass the time.

As they stood there, a couple walked past and the woman said to Dean, "Hey, Dean! Deano, is that you?"

He had his head turned away and didn't seem to hear her at first, but then slowly turned and looked a little startled.

"Oh, Joyce, um, hi. How are you? What in the world are you doing up here? Never thought I'd run into you up *here,* heh, heh." Dean said nervously.

She turned to her companion who was carrying two plates of food and said, "Look, Denny, it's Dean. And hey, here's Karla. Hi Karla!" giving her a hug with one arm.

Denny said, "Wow, what the hell are you guys doin' up here in the cold? We heard you went and moved to Virginia when they finished that big CIA installation you were always waiting for. Watch this…big change in administration makin' it too hot down in D.C. for ya? Ha, ha, ha."

"Well, uh, we did go for awhile, but we… we came back," said Dean. "Retired and in New York State now. Uh, huh, just a retired nobody now, heh, heh."

"Good, good," Denny said. "Yes, real good…yup, yeah, ah…good then…"

There was an awkward length of time when no one said anything. Shawn and Amy expected to be introduced to these old friends of their two new friends, but for some reason, it never happened. Dean just quit talking and looked away. Denny and Joyce cleared their throats, nodded at Shawn and Amy, then slowly moved toward the overlook with plates in hand and puzzled looks on their faces.

Shawn and Amy smiled and nodded wondering what had just happened.

Dean turned to Shawn and said, "Old neighbors, nice people, nice people. We use to ride with them a while ago. Never expected to see them up here…or anywhere… *ah*, in the snow. Nope, a *real* surprise, huh Karla?"

Karla smiled and said, "Yeah, they were nice. Really good seeing them again. Um, maybe you should go back and talk with them awhile. You know, t*alk* with them a while, Dean."

But by now, their food was ready. After they picked up their plates of hamburgers and hot dogs and exited the line, Shawn slowed. He sensed something was amiss. It was probably their fault these old friends were not re-acquainting. Dean and Karla might feel that they should hang around with Shawn and Amy, even though they would probably never see each other again.

"You guys go ahead and sit with your old friends. We're gonna cozy-up by the fire and eat. I'm sure you've got a lot to talk about," Shawn said.

Dean said, "Well, no, actually, we'd rather eat with you two. They're way over by the ledge. We'll just stay with you guys… if that's alright? We'll say good-bye to them when we leave. Besides, we have to show you the way back, right?"

"Well, thanks but we're gonna eat fast and keep going farther out for awhile," said Shawn, letting him know they were not interested in keeping company with them anymore. "We only have today. We're going home tomorrow. I'd rather put on some more miles. But hey, thanks, and it's been a pleasure meeting you two. Have a safe ride back," as he shook Dean's free hand.

"Well, alright then, I…I guess…I won't insist. Thanks for coming along. We might not have come up by ourselves," Dean said with a slight smile and a puzzled look.

Karla added to Amy, "That GPS is about three hundred dollars. It'll make a great gift for somebody looking *not* to get lost," she winked at Shawn.

"Hey, thanks for the tip," Amy responded, "And take care. Bye. Be careful."

After they walked away Shawn and Amy sat on a log near the fire.

"Why'd ya do that?" asked Amy.

"Do what?" Shawn replied, biting into the burger.

"You know, blow them off like that."

"I don't know what you mean."

"Come on, Shawn. They seemed like nice people. Why not ride with them?"

"We *did* ride with them."

"You know what I mean."

"Huh, uh."

"You do too," she said.

Shawn swallowed, wiped his mouth and was quiet for about twenty seconds.

"You know how we always talk about Bill and stuff? You know all the good times we had with our old friends? All the good rides and that. You know?" he asked.

"Well, sure," said Amy softly.

"Well, every time we do, it takes a little piece out of me. I mean, I really long for those good times to happen again, but with those *same* people... again. But I know they won't, they can't...*ever*," Shawn said turning away from Amy.

"Don't you ever want to ride with new people, Shawn?" Amy said softly. "They might be fun to be with, too. You know?"

"Yeah, I know, I know," Shawn frowned. "But it can never be quite the same. Maybe I just don't want to get too friendly with new people. Or maybe I'm just afraid I'm getting old and I can't stop the clock. Or maybe they're too old. How long are they going to ride anyway, do you know? We'd get to be friendly and they'd kick, or something would happen and like their other friends over there, they'd quit riding with us and we'd be here by ourselves again anyway. It takes something out of me. I'm telling you, I don't know why, it just does and I don't like it. It's a lot worse since I got back. Sorry, Amy."

"I can understand that, Shawn. Maybe after a while things will get better. You know, time takes care of a lot of things. Puts a lot of things back into proper perspective," she said and rubbed his shoulder.

"I guess," Shawn replied. "Right now I just want to enjoy us two being together, out here on our sleds, today. I'll think about all that other stuff tomorrow."

They finished lunch, waved a good-bye to Dean, Karla and friends and mounted their sleds.

On the way to the main trail they each thought that their old group never got to do anything quite like this, they surely would have loved it.

Shawn frowned and then smiled as he opened the throttle after completing the turn in the opposite direction they had come in from. They rode quickly up the mountain side, enjoying once again the performance of their snowmobiles, especially Shawn on the XMZ. He loved the way it carved up the switchbacks the sweeping mountain road offered up.

As they climbed a long side hill trail, Shawn slowed and looked back down. He could see at least two miles down their backtrail. He saw a group of sleds, six black with two blue ones in the lead, moving quickly up the mountain side. He thought it must be a club or a dealer expedition.

They were out perhaps 40 miles from the cook-out, and riding on some poorly marked and deteriorated trails. The wide, smooth, logging roads had disappeared miles ago. Shawn stopped at a junction with an even older trail, to look at the map.

"Hey, Amy, what do you think? Pretty bumpy huh?" Shawn asked.

"Yeah. Hey, I'm gonna take a pee here. Watch for me," as she took several tissues from her storage bin in the rear of the sled.

"Okay, I'm gonna check out another way back."

Amy picked a place fifty feet from the trail behind a large downed tree as Shawn perused the map.

When she got back she said, "That's better!" and added, "What's up?"

"Well, I'm not sure. I think this is where we are... here," he poked his finger at a crossroad on the map. "If I had a GPS I guess I'd know for sure, huh?"

"Yup, so buy one, I don't care. You can have that for your birthday then. Saves me from shopping for the wrong thing, huh?"

"Yeah, that'll work for me, hun. I think we can cut across this trail here and save an hour or two," he pointed to the narrow trail next to his sled.

"It doesn't look like they ever groom it, Shawn... You sure?" Amy questioned.

"I don't know... It shows it as a club trail. Maybe no one's been on it since the last snow."

"Well, if it doesn't get any better, I vote we turn around and go back the way we came. It may be longer but we know it's open and clear. It's getting a little late."

"Okay," said Shawn as he started his engine.

The old trail was deep with untouched snow. There were a lot of low hanging limbs, a definite sign that no one had pruned it this season, or maybe even last. Lack of pruning sometimes indicated a trail is closed for some reason. But Shawn still believed his read was correct. It would save them miles and much time, and it did have the old generation, yellow diamond markers nailed to occasional trees indicating snowmobile usage permitted.

After five very slow miles, they experienced a series of places where they had to turn off the trail to skirt downed trees. Some of them had probably been there for years. Amy really wanted Shawn to give it up and go back to the main trail, but he was trying to maintain enough forward speed to keep his big engine cool. He wouldn't stop long enough to allow her to tell him she wanted to go back, *now!*

She hated it when he did this. She believed he knew full well she was getting upset but he would continue stubbornly on to prove he was correct.

Shawn swooped down a hill to the left and picked up even more speed in the pristine snow. Amy was still at the top when Shawn crossed a low lying section that was flat but rather narrow. Off to his right there was a cleared area about a hundred feet in diameter and to the left a slight drop off. He stayed on the flat and narrow portion and headed for an open spot in the woods.

About eighty feet from the woods he hit a mushy section and his sled bottomed out. He gave it more throttle and just managed to power through. Once past, he coasted to a stop and turned and looked back to make sure Amy didn't hit the same spot he had at too fast a speed.

He noticed Amy was off to his right about twenty feet from where the soft spot was. For some reason she chose not to stay in his tracks. Her sled bogged down even more than Shawn's had as it struggled in the mushy wet stuff. It lost forward speed rapidly, and then finally stopped. Suddenly the rear of her sled sank two feet. She was sinking into a beaver pond!

Shawn gasped and yelled, "*NO!*"

Amy reacted quickly and stepped off to her right and up onto the snow covered pond. Her sled was still running and the headlight was pointed skyward at a forty-five degree angle.

Shawn ran toward her and wondered why she went that way.

He stood just before the soft spot on what he now knew was the breast of a beaver dam. He told Amy to stay put for a second but she would have none of it. She galloped off the frozen pond. Shawn held out his hand, Amy ignored it.

"What the hell are you doing, Shawn?" Amy yelled at him.

"What the hell am I doing?" Shawn replied. "No...It's what the hell are *you* doing? Why'd ya go on the pond?" He added.

"Why didn't you turn around like you said you would, Shawn?" she asked. "Why are you going so damned fast?"

"'Cause we're saving time and miles going this way, Amy, get it?" Shawn said.

"Oh, yeah, I get it. Just look at how much time we're saving. I can't wait to see how quickly you get my sled out," she pointed at her idling snowmobile.

"You can never admit any blame, huh, Amy? It's always someone else's fault, huh? You still haven't said why you went on the lake," Shawn yelled. "It's not like you can't tell there's water there."

Amy flipped up her face shield and yelled back, "'Cause I did! And don't say you knew it was a pond, Shawn. Admit it, you didn't. I know you didn't know. You're so cautious you'd stop way before ever going over a dam. Right, Shawn? You're not fooling me, bud. I know you way too well."

Shawn said in a calmer voice, "Well, I thought it was. Right before I turned and saw you way out there," he pointed to the sled, now with the water line up and over the glowing rear tail light. "You all right?" Shawn added calmly.

"My foot is wet. I bet all my stuff is wet now. It's all in my trunk."

"We'll get socks from my sled. Did the ice seem okay where you stepped off?"

"I suppose so. I wouldn't go too far out, though. It could be deep."

"Well, I have to get the rope on it somehow, Amy." Shawn said as he walked back and removed the tow strap from Jay's snowmobile trunk.

Gingerly, he stepped out onto the snow covered ice, ahead of where the sled sat idling. He wasn't certain how deep the water was. It could easily be over his head. He knelt down and, stretching, carefully placed the double spring hooks onto the tips of Amy's skis. Slowly, he backed away until he was once again next to the XMZ. He attached the other end of the thirty foot nylon strap to his sled and wrapped it once about the rear bumper, hooking it to itself. He mounted his sled.

Shawn inched his sled forward until the slack was out of the tow strap and then opened the throttle. The carbide studded track tried to grip the surface, but spun uselessly, digging down several inches and sending twigs and mud flying. He reversed to take some of the tautness out of the tow rope and once again hit the throttle. It didn't move Amy's sled; just dug itself down into the muddy ground beneath the snow.

Shawn got off his sled and stood staring at the half submerged problem still dutifully running. He couldn't imagine how he was going to pull it out of the pond without some help. As Shawn studied the dilemma, he realized that even if he could manage to pull Amy's sled forward, it would more than likely slide under the ice because of the fulcrum point of the skis.

Suddenly, Amy stepped out onto the ice and motioned for Shawn to get back on his sled. Shawn shook his head no; Amy gestured and refused to leave her sled. Finally, reluctantly, Shawn straddled the XMZ's seat.

He looked back at Amy, precariously perched on one foot; the other on the end of the right ski, bending the tip down toward the ice. Her left hand was gripping the throttle, ready to open it up and help it climb out of the hole.

Shawn didn't wait any longer. He gave his sled half throttle. Amy's plan worked and the little red sled that could popped out of its resting place and moved toward the dam. Amy slipped onto her snowmobile and joined Shawn on the shore. She raised her hands high in the sky for victory.

She shouted, "Yes, yes!"

Shawn gave her a hug and patted her on the back.

Amy smiled that special smile that came when she had accomplished a real achievement and opened the trunk to see how wet things were. She gave a slight scream, took off her gloves and scooped two very sluggish and surprised tadpoles from the trunk.

She threw them back into the hole in the pond.

"Get outta here! It's too early. You're not even supposed to be around here in winter."

Finding that the plastic bag that held her extra pair of dry socks was full of water, she signaled for Shawn to give her his. He rummaged in his trunk and handed her the bag.

He said, "Ya know, someone told me one time, we should pack my stuff in your sled and your stuff in mine, just in case something like this happened."

"What? Now you're blaming me for not having dry stuff to wear? Why didn't you say something earlier if it was such a good idea? And it is." She was apparently not interested in sharing any 'up-beat' moments with Shawn.

"I'm not blaming you; can't you take a little good advice?" he said.

Amy dried off her foot with some paper towels and said, "Here's some good advice for you. Turn around. I don't want to ride this trail anymore. Just turn around."

Shawn pleaded, "OK, I will, just one more mile. Just one and if it doesn't get better we can go back. We ought to be real close, Amy. Promise."

"Close to what, Shawn? Close to *what?* What's out here but more of what we've seen all day long? It's beautiful but..." she stopped. "Is there something you want to tell me, Shawn? Shawn?"

"Um, well, ah... Jay said there is this spectacular vista out here that's a must see. He said there is nothing else like it. I kind of promised I'd get us there. Come on, Amy, we might never get back here. Remember what we talked about last night?"

She just looked at him for a while, then said, "Ah, man. Oh, all right. I guess." She shook her head.

They packed all the dry stuff back into Shawn's sled.

After they left the breast of the dam, Amy saw water squirting out of the front of her seat with each bump she hit. She thought even with her expensive suit it was just a matter of time until she would be soaked. Shawn, while he appreciated her acceptance of another mile, didn't look back to check on her.

As they came out of the woods they found an old logging road. Amy thought Shawn would stop, but with the clear roadway in front of him, he picked up speed and she couldn't pull beside him. They had ridden about two miles before she managed to overtake and signal for him to stop. He glided to a halt and Amy pulled directly behind him.

"What the hell are you doing?" she shouted. "I thought you'd at least turn around to see if I'm okay. So what do you do? You keep going like a jerk. Thanks for that, Shawn. Sometimes you just don't care what I want, do you? What happens to me?"

He knew that she knew that he did it to prove that he could. That he read the map correctly and he was capable of finding his way around even when others might doubt him.

"What the hell, Amy," Shawn shouted back at her. "I think I know where I am. And we'll get back just fine. So quit whining."

"I'm all wet, Shawn. My butt's all wet... *Look!*" she said as she turned around.

"I don't know what I can do about that. Can you make it back if it's about two hours?"

"I'm okay on the seat... I guess. But if it gets bumpy and I have to stand up I can feel it getting really cold. I'm afraid of frostbite."

"Well, I think we can ride these old logging roads back. You'll be able to sit most of the way. And we can move along pretty good. We'll skip the overlook, ok?"

"Go. Just go. I don't care right now... Whatever," Amy responded.

Shawn turned back around and when he did he noticed an old concrete building off to his left, in the distance. There was smoke coming out of a small chimney. It was about an eighth of a mile away and down in a thinly forested, previously strip-mined, area. He wished Amy wasn't wet, and that they had more time; it would make a neat side trip to check out an unexpected piece of industrial archeology, something Shawn had appreciated for a long time.

Then he noticed some activity. As he watched, he saw one, and then two, then six people exit the small door in front. They ran to some tarped snowmobiles and quickly removed the covers. He wondered what was going on; was it some sort of emergency?

Suddenly, the garage door was flung open and out came a big, black snowmobile with sparkling red and gold graphics. It looked just like the one Shawn was riding. It accelerated rapidly toward where Shawn and Amy sat, throwing up a massive rooster tail in its wake.

Suddenly they heard "spinnggg," "wap" and then some more sounds unfamiliar to Amy, but all too familiar to Shawn. A nearby tree limb exploded and wood splinters filled the air.

"Oh my God," Shawn yelled. "They're shooting at us. What the hell?"

Amy was stunned. She couldn't move. This must not be happening. This must be a bad dream.

Shawn thought that for whatever reason, these people were serious and they had better get moving. Apparently they were not asking questions first; those were live rounds; they were actually shooting at them. He remembered that the attendant he hurt had said he would kill Shawn; it gave him a sinking feeling in his stomach.

THE CHASE

He motioned for Amy to quickly go in front of him, but she acted like a deer caught in the headlights; unable to take her eyes off of the sleds getting nearer.

Shawn screamed at her, "Amy! *Amy!* Go! NOW*!!*"

She suddenly snapped out of her stupor and hit the throttle only to run into the back of Shawn's sled. He dared not wait any longer for her get in front of him. She would have to try to keep up. Shawn opened full throttle and the front of his sled rose sharply in the air. Amy's did the same. Both sleds came back down on the snow as Shawn and Amy took off into unfamiliar territory, running for their lives.

There was apparently no point in trying to talk to these guys, Amy quickly realized, as she hunched down on the seat of her flying sled. It was escape or be killed. Why did Jay insist on them coming this way? Who are these people and why the hell are they doing this? They weren't looking for trouble. They were just passing through.

The old logging road offered no cover, but did allow them to create an early, sizable gap between them and their pursuers. Shawn remembered an article he had read in an old car magazine written by a reporter who had taken a ride in an F-14 Tom Cat fighter jet. When the pilot took them down to ground level through a gunnery range, the reporter was amazed at how quickly his eyes adjusted. As they passed by large southern pine trees at 200 plus miles per hour the reporter commented on his ability to actually see, for a micro second, the shape, color and texture of the bark on a particular tree he looked at.

Shawn was experiencing that very same phenomenon as he glimpsed the trees he was flying past. *The consummate observer*, he thought to himself. They were in a street fight here, a bad one. He would have to rely on his military experience. He just hoped it would be enough.

They had traveled several very fast miles and Shawn's hands were sweating profusely, making the inside of his gloves wet and slippery. He kept shoving his hands forward so his gloves would not slip off the throttle and grips. Every chance he got, he turned back to make sure Amy was still behind him. He knew actually stopping her would be difficult because she was moving fast. She could be a real fighter if cornered.

Shooting a gun at these speeds? It was something Shawn believed they couldn't do with any accuracy. And, ah yes, a gun. Why did Amy insist, and he accept, not bringing a side arm? Of all the rides they had ever had, when it wasn't needed, he had it along. This would be the trip he really did need it and didn't have it. How stupid. *Wouldn't you know it,* he thought, *the one time he was really right might be the last time they ever see each other.*

Shawn was scared; even in Iraq he didn't feel this vulnerable. He kept his eyes on the road except to take a quick glance back to make sure Amy was keeping up. Riding at this speed on the unfamiliar sled and trying to figure out how to get them out of this situation was terrifying.

Amy couldn't see any headlights but she knew they were coming. It would have to be the fastest ride of their lives if they were to escape this. What if they couldn't get away? Was this God's payback for her cheating on Shawn?

She only did it the one time and now this? Maybe Shawn had been right about the gun. She hoped she would have the opportunity to tell him it was partly her fault, especially the cheating, and that she still loved him and wanted everything to work out okay between them.

It was getting dark quickly and the logging road ended abruptly. As Shawn rounded the bend and entered into a field under wide opened throttle, the big sled ran perfectly. This was the ride of his life. Too bad he wasn't able to enjoy it.

They approached another wooded section of the trail. Shawn was traveling fast, very fast—probably 80 miles per hour—he didn't dare look. He hoped Amy could somehow keep up until they reached somewhere safe; a village, a bar, maybe a gas station. He had no way of knowing what lay ahead.

He had his butt way off the seat; his hands worked the bars quickly back and forth to keep the sliding 600 pound mass pointed in approximately the right direction. Heart pounding, stomach feeling light, he dropped down a slight hill to the right and then the dark icy trail took an unexpectedly sharp turn to the left. A narrow, sloping, twenty foot long wooden bridge appeared in his peripheral vision. Physics and the sled tried to counter his steering input and stay on a straight path. Shawn fought to override and correct for it but he was going way too fast.

As he pulled hard on the brake lever, the sled over corrected and passed onto the leading edge of the bridge in a slide. The rubber track clawed at the sides and he saw bright yellow and red sparks flying as the carbide studs did their job, scratching and grinding on unsuspecting nails and bolts. Just as the sled started to straighten out on the structure and Shawn began to think he had the situation in hand, he felt the bottom give way. The sled pitched into a nose dive and he was a helpless passenger. No amount of jockeying could have an effect from here on and he knew it.

The bridge snapped cleanly in half as if it had been cut; the front portion tipped downward but the far end held almost level. Shawn slammed the edge of the remaining structure with his chest while the sled slid under it. It all happened fast, but it felt like slow motion to Shawn. Even the pain took time to reach his brain after he lost his breath and heard bone and cartilage being crushed together.

Shawn folded at the waist.

He was lucky in a way that he didn't stay on the sled. It slammed into the far wall of the chasm. Shawn instinctively tried to grab part of the dangling bridge but he couldn't hold on. He briefly lost consciousness and fell ten feet onto a ledge on the side of the gorge. Part of his suit ripped off and fluttered from some jagged boards.

He tumbled onto his back, gasping for air and looked up only to see flashes of light dancing across the tops of the trees. It was Amy!

Shawn tried to move but couldn't as the sound of her engine grew louder. She would hit the bridge and get hurt, he thought, as he struggled to turn over.

Coming off the field at nearly the same speed as Shawn, Amy took the right turn down the hill just as Shawn had. Her rear end was way off the seat to counteract the centrifugal force. She, too, was going much too fast and approached the bridge at a skewed angle. But her lighter sled responded differently than Shawn's. It straightened earlier, early enough, in fact, for her headlight to catch a glimpse of reflective tape she had sewn on the front of Shawn's snowmobile suit. She could see it dangling low in the dark woods, giving her a clue that something was terribly wrong.

She jammed on the brakes and her sled began to slide. She couldn't see the edge of the bridge, so she simply held the brake on as hard as she could. As her track bit and jerked to a stop, it snapped her to the left and catapulted her from the seat. Her snowmobile hit a large pine tree, rolled over, and stopped on an angle. She hit some low pine boughs and slid off the edge of the rocky trail about fifteen feet from the gorge. She rolled down the incline and finally stopped with her feet hanging over the precipice. She was semi-conscious and hurt.

Barely aware of her surroundings, she could hear her sled but couldn't see it on the other side of the tree. The throttle was stuck open, engine screaming; then silence. Where was Shawn? She could see the far side of the fallen bridge but didn't see him or his sled.

She frantically called for him through her closed face shield but only a hoarse whisper came out.

Even if Shawn had heard Amy, he couldn't have answered her. She called him repeatedly, the last time her voice drowned out by the sound of snowmobile engines entering the woods behind her.

She saw the lights and screamed, "You bastards!"

She turned back toward the bridge; her main concern was Shawn. What had happened to him? She yelled his name over and over again and hoped to hear something... *anything*. Then she laid still. The snow hadn't yet penetrated her insulated suit. She thought maybe if the men chasing them didn't see her, they would leave and she could find Shawn.

Shawn, too, heard the sleds and dragged himself across the ledge. He tried to pull himself up by shear strength and force of will. The pain in his chest was excruciating. He was badly hurt and he couldn't move his legs. But he was desperate to make sure Amy was okay.

Using his arms, Shawn managed to grasp some brush growing from the side of the sloping wall of the chasm. Pulling himself painfully up to the rim, he lay gasping for breath.

The men stood talking about thirty feet away. They were on the other side of a thicket. Shawn couldn't make out what they were saying but they didn't seem to be in a hurry to do anything. It was almost as if they knew that the game they pursued was already in the bag.

Suddenly the sounds of the idling sleds diminished as they were, one after another, turned off. Shawn noticed movement to his right. A small grey squirrel stopped about five feet from his face, and then darted into the end of a massive, hollow pine tree. The opening was about two feet in diameter.

Shawn knew he needed to find cover. As quietly as he could, he pulled his battered body into the dark tree trunk. He rested once he thought he had gotten his body within the hiding spot. Some feeling seemed to be coming back into his legs. Sharp, searing jolts of pain shot down the backs of both legs. It took all his control to keep from crying out.

Shawn watched as the squirrel was silhouetted bounding toward the far end of the trunk, maybe twenty feet away. If he could crawl to the other end, closer to where the men were talking, maybe he could hear what they were planning.

He forced his way deeper into the rotted log, the smell of animal urine and moss hanging heavily in the air. Shawn didn't want to think about what was sharing the inside of the log with him. He pulled himself forward a few inches at a time, using his hands and forearms and pushing with his feet. At first it seemed impossible, the air was almost unbearable to breathe and he kept getting snagged by sharp splinters of wood.

He began to think about getting stuck in this old, coffin-like log and dying in it, unnoticed and alone, maybe only to be found when the outside had rotted away and exposed him—or what was left of him.

Finally, after several pain-filled minutes, the opening was close.

As he rested, Shawn saw the squirrel near the end of the log watching him. Shawn thought about when he was 18 and he and a neighbor were rabbit hunting on a farm in Western Pennsylvania. Not having seen any game for hours and tired of walking the fields they stopped in a wooded area to rest. His friend lit a cigarette; Shawn stood with his gun at his side about ten feet away at the other end of a rotting log.

After nearly finishing his cigarette, the friend bent over at his end of the log. He stood upright, cigarette dangling from his smiling mouth, and turned toward Shawn. He said in a monotone, matter-of-fact manner, "There's one in here. There's a rabbit in this log here," pointing at the end of the log.

Shawn chuckled and said, "Yeah, right."

"Look, I'll poke 'em and you can shoot 'em. He's all yours."

Shawn stopped grinning and said, "You're shitin' me, right?"

"Nope. Get ready and I'll kick em' out."

Shawn didn't think he was being told the truth so he half heartedly stood at attention; his right hand loosely holding the stock of his single shot, full choke, Harrington/Richardson .410 shotgun.

His buddy nodded in a questioning manner and Shawn nodded back. Just then the friend gave the rotted log a firm kick. It sounded like a pumpkin smashing on the ground. *Kawoomp!*

Instantly, the harried hare blasted out of Shawn's end of the log, running a narrow, zigzag pattern. Shawn was shocked and caught off guard. He fumbled as he pulled the hammer back and aimed where he thought the quick, little furry bullet was headed. But he pulled the trigger far too quickly, setting him back on his heels. The silence was shattered and brown 'puffer balls' hidden under the dried leaves spewed spores into the air and twigs scattered widely. He missed the rabbit but gouged a dark, three foot oval trough into the damp forest floor.

After the rabbit disappeared into the mountain laurel both of the great white hunters slowly looked toward each other with cocked heads. Then, without words, they shrugged and started back out into the fields.

Shawn momentarily broke into a smile. Then he remembered the situation he was currently in and it immediately sobered him.

Lying just inside the hollow log, Shawn could hear the conversation more clearly. Someone must have been on a cell or satellite phone.

"Worked great…Thanks. Ya sent 'em right to our front door. Ha, ha, yeah. Yeah… Well, he wrecked it. Someone sabotaged the bridge… No damned good to us now… I don't know… You gotta send up another one… And now… They want even more of them…(long pause) No… *Now I said, NOW!* Better figure another way then. Pack up a truck… I don't care, just get some more fast sleds up here. No, I don't know *where* he is yet… I told you the girl would probably make it… If you want her to… But I think he's done for… Can't see him comin' back out of that ditch… Sled's gone, too… Like I said, he just trashed it. What a waste. What a waste."

He continued, "Well, they won't tell me much. They still need five more fast sleds, I do know that. It'll take me a couple more weeks and then I'm done with this, you know. We're still putting on the launchers. Guess I'll have to stock pile 'em here until they give me the signal the raid is on… I don't know about the C-4, I don't want to screw with that stuff… And there's another big, heavy box they delivered, all wrapped up in plastic and warnings. Got special seals all over it. Say's not to open it and they'd need it well protected and on its own little trailer too. Not sure what the hell *that* is. Shit, I don't *want* to know.

"Ya know, they'd probably kill me if I ask too many questions or think too much. You're an Arab or something, aren't ya? You know they carry *real* AK's? … No, I don't care about 'the cause,' your 'jihad' or whatever, I just want the rest of my money and I'm gone. I told you before, as far as I'm concerned, they're payin' good, and most up front, too. I'm not gonna piss anyone off by this deal here today. I want to keep it that way, hear me? Now, what do ya want me to do with your 'cutie pie' here, huh? Sure, Jay, I can make it look like it was a tree if you want it that way. Alright... Yeah... Sure. Maybe I *will* have some fun first, we'll see. I'll let you know if I liked it...Yeah she is... Okay."

Shawn froze as the man moved closer to the opening. He stared as he saw his boots just inches away. He had seen these boots before. They had neat little holes punched in the top.

Just then another squirrel, apparently trapped inside by Shawn, scampered over his shoulder, out of the log and into the open.

"Whoa!" the man outside yelled aloud.

Crack! Crack! Shawn heard as someone tried to shoot it.

"Oh!" Shawn moaned, ears ringing.

He inhaled sharply and coughed; noise, he had just made some noise. Shawn lay frozen. He stared at the end of the log, afraid to pull back.

The boots turned slowly toward the log. The end of the log darkened and Shawn saw a face appear about two feet away.

It was Markus. Markus! He stood up and laughed loudly.

"Oh yeah, lookie here boys," he shouted to the others and kicked the log, sending splinters into Shawn's eyes and mouth.

What now? Beg for mercy? Crawl out? Plead? What? Shawn couldn't think. He couldn't talk. He couldn't react. He just stared at some old, burned tree stumps fifty feet away that looked to him like tombstones covered with marshmallow sauce and pondered his fate. After all he had been through in Iraq, he never expected to have a marshmallow tombstone as his grave marker.

Markus stood up and yelled over his shoulder.

"Hey, Bruno...Here, this one's yours. You owe him. I'll go do the girl."

 He turned and walked away. Then Shawn saw the groper from the bar. He walked directly toward Shawn's hideout; grinning every step of the way. He was carrying a large bore hunting rifle. Shawn started to pray.

Bruno pulled up his gun, cocked it and began to aim it toward Shawn's face.

Suddenly, all hell broke loose. Shawn heard a tremendous commotion; rustling and yelling everywhere.

Pop! Pop! Pop! Bruno fell, writhing on the ground.

Shawn took a deep breath, thinking he had been shot, waiting for the pain.

There was more shooting and shouting. Smoke, noise and the all too familiar smell of cosmoline; it was thick. The log vibrated from the concussion of very powerful, automatic weapons being fired nearby. *Rat-a-tat! rat-a-tat! rat-a-tat!* It hurt Shawn's ears and made them ring. It seemed to last a lifetime!

It was Iraq all over again!

Then it stopped just as suddenly as it had started. Shawn lay still for several minutes, just listening and barely breathing. He still expected to feel something painful, some burning somewhere on his body to indicate he had been wounded from shrapnel.

Shawn heard new voices and, faintly, a helicopter. What the hell had just happened? He cried out, "Amy!"

Someone heard him and stooped down in front of the log. "Holy shit, sir. Look at this."

It was a Canadian Mounty dressed in white coveralls, gloves, boots and helmet. His gun was even white. Quickly, he kneeled down and reached into the log and pulled Shawn out. He carefully propped him against a nearby tree, guarding him as if he were the enemy.

Shawn moaned. He was still in pain from the wreck. He looked around, obviously dazed. He kept wiping at his face, trying to get the wood dust and mold spores out of his eyes and nose. He coughed and spit attempting to clear the rotting pulp from his mouth.

He saw Amy about thirty feet away, propped against a tree. She was receiving medical assistance and she managed to wave to Shawn. She had a wan smile on her face. Karla was kneeling beside her.

Another Canadian Mounty in white, Dean and two men in black military boots and jumpsuits with U.S. Homeland Security badges dangling in the front came over to Shawn and apologized for bringing them into the situation. They pushed the guard's gun down and away from him.

One squatted down and patted Shawn on the shoulder.

"We're sorry to have put you in this place, son. These guys were bad. Bad for our country and bad for theirs," he nodded toward the Mounty. "We bugged your machine along the roadway; remember the stop? We knew Jay sent you up here. We had to find them this way. We *had* to do this. There was no other choice; not enough time left. They had been stealing snowmobiles for months and shipping them up here. Your buddy, Jay? Part of a major terrorist plot to attack Fort Drum using snowmobiles loaded with C-4 and rocket launchers. And maybe some other really bad stuff. You and Amy should be very proud. You helped stop a huge attack on your government, your homeland. You'll get a promotion at least for this, son, I'm certain."

The guard added with a smile on his face, "Cool. You might get a medal too, eh?"

Shawn groaned, slumped down and closed his eyes. He was exhausted.

Seconds later, he coughed, grimaced and said to the guard and the two H.S. agents in a whisper, "Yeah, real cool. You almost got us killed here." He paused. "Yeah, I know, I know…The Hum-Vee's, the fishing hut, Dean's sled. All those black sleds, I know, I've been in Special Forces, right? I've got eyes. I knew *something* was up. But this? Not this."

The H.S. agent said, "Well, we did contact you, just to give you a hint something was up. To keep your eyes open. You should have gotten a special delivery notification a day or so ago."

The other HS agent chimed in, "You weren't alone, son. Your neighbor Hawkins…the guy staying next to you at the Inn. With them, our chopper and our drone, we had you covered like a cheap suit, Shawn. We knew when you left home, where you were and what you were doing every second of the day, except during that damned blizzard. We weren't going to let you get hurt, well, not badly, not if we could help it. You'll be okay, now…You did good, Shawn, *real* good."

Shawn said, "You said Jay? You can't mean Jay Shamal, though. He's a good friend. I've known him for years. He couldn't hurt his country."

One agent from H.S. stood and dialed a phone while the other knelt by Shawn.

"Sorry, Shawn. He didn't try to hurt his country. Jay is not an American; never was. He didn't enter this country legally. He has always been and always will be a Syrian soldier. A lot of them are good people I suppose, but he just decided to get involved with a bad bunch of fanatics.

Did you know his name is really Jabr Shamal? Over there it means something like 'Commander of the North Winds'. Maybe he thought he'd abuse your relationship, you know, your Mid-Eastern ancestry and attempt something big for the fanatics back home. Maybe live up to his nickname...Who knows? Don't forget he tricked you into delivering that big sled for him, son. Would a real friend do something like that?"

He continued, "Now, Markus, well... He thought that his little wilderness 'country' was more important than our whole, big country. He saw a chance to make some real big money and took it. He was a traitor, plain and simple. Will they miss him at the camp? I'm sure they will, but they'll get along."

The other agent closed his satellite phone and said, "Yeah, Walt just arrested Shamal."

"Surprised?" the agent asked.

"Ha! Extremely surprised. Tried to blow himself up."

As they strapped Shawn onto a stretcher, they brought Amy over beside him. She was strapped onto her own.

The agent's phone rang and after a few seconds he handed it to Shawn. "For you."

"Me?" Shawn said softly. "Uh, hello? Major? Oh, um, yes. Oh yes, Major Cole. Thank you, sir…Yes sir…. You're kidding. Are you *serious*, sir? Yes, sir. You are? Oh yeah? I am? Yes, sir. Six weeks, sir? Yes, I will, sir. Thank you, sir. Good bye, sir."

Shawn closed the phone and handed it back to the agent.

"Major Cole, Amy," he said, smiling. "He's really proud of me. It ended the way it's supposed to. All the bad guys down, all the good guys up and around. He said I never left my unit. They helped set this up but couldn't say anything to me…Couldn't tell me. He called my part of the operation 'Hotel California'…Ha, one of my faves. Makes some sense, now, I guess. I thought I checked out of my unit but never really left. They knew that I knew Jay pretty well and figured he might try to use me for this. What a jerk. Shamal. I thought he was a friend."

He coughed hard, winced and took a long breath and continued in a whisper, "I'm getting a promotion to Captain, Amy, and they will get all of my pay to us within a week. They were holding it. He apologized to you, too… Hopes you're okay. They never did have a problem with me, Amy. I was still working all along and didn't know it. I was still serving my country. Wow, I feel great. Just great," he coughed as a tear tracked down his cheek.

Looking over without lifting her head she said in a whisper, "Hey, that's just super, Shawn. That's great, babe. And, ah, some real nice riding there, champ."

She garnered a glance from one of the medics that checked her gurney hold-down straps. "I guess you weren't so bad yourself, young lady."

Shawn replied, "And the next time, stay off my fat butt. Okay?"

Amy snickered.

"Sure, bucco, you name it. Love you."

"Love you, too…For always, Amy."

They reached out and grasped each other's hands as the medics struggled to carry them that way to the waiting MEDIVAC helicopter.

As they left the ground, Amy said, "Well, I can sure say I'll never forget *this* ride, Shawn. How 'bout you?" Then she added, "I hope this thing is fast, bucco. I'm gonna need a pit stop…*And soon*, that's for sure."

Shawn just smiled and said, "My kidneys are just killing me, Amy… Maybe you were right all along."

EPILOGUE

Shawn stared out of the second floor window at some kids playing in the hot, sun-filled, dirt courtyard. He was conflicted and his emotions were wreaking havoc. There was a gnawing sense of unfinished business; a common feeling that affected some soldiers when they left the battle zone. It was a sadness that, unless you had been there, most people couldn't understand. A lot of soldiers were drawn back in, wanting to somehow finish their part of the job.

After the sting he was involved in back home, Shawn didn't expect or want to come back to the war zone. With the fighting still underway in Afghanistan, however, being a hero of sorts didn't stop his redeployment after recovering from his injuries in Canada. He had put in a complete tour this time and today he was leaving Iraq for good.

Shawn was questioning his desire to leave and wasn't sure how to handle it. His first tour in Iraq had been cut short because, unbeknownst to him, he was to be a decoy in a sting operation to catch some terrorists threatening the United States homeland. But this was his own decision; one he thought would be easy. Now, however, he wondered what would happen here after he was gone.

"Captain Kaan, sir?" the Corporal said from the open doorway "Your car is here to take you to the airport. Your flight home, sir?"

"Oh, uh… Thank you, Corporal," he continued to look out of the window.

"Yes sir…You're welcome, sir."

"Corporal?" Shawn said to the twenty-something man.

"Yes sir?"

"Have any kids?"

"Ah, no, sir. Not yet, sir. But planning on it after I get home, sir. You, sir?"

"Yeah, a new one," Shawn said smiling. "Shawna. She's three months now. Haven't seen her yet. Will soon though. She's my little Conair baby."

"That's nice, sir. Great, ah, what's a Conair baby, sir? You *did it* on a plane, sir? I'm sorry, sir. Just asking."

"It's a long story, Corporal, a *very* long story. And, ah, no, it's a hair dryer—Conair—it's a brand of hair dryer, not the prisoner plane."

"Yes, sir, a hair dryer it is, sir. No plane, sir."

"Corporal?"

"Yes, sir?"

"We know a lot of those little guys down there, right? Nice kids, and friendly, you know?

"Yes, sir, they really are… Very nice kids, sir."

"Do you think these kids will grow up to hate our kids?"

"I don't know, sir. I hope not. I hope not, sir."

"Me, too, Corporal, me, too. Do you think we did the right thing here?"

"Sir? Not sure what you mean, sir."

"Do you think we've damaged this place more than we've helped it?"

"I don't know, sir. It was pretty bad when we came here, sir."

"Yeah, I guess so. Probably helped more than we know then, huh?"

"Yes, sir…I'm sure we've helped a great deal, sir. The car, sir?" the Corporal said and picked up Shawn's duffle bag off of the floor.

"Ah, yes, time to leave once again," Shawn sighed.

He picked up his attaché case and, with one last look out the window and another sigh, he touched his desk with his fingers and strode through the doorway.

He stopped several yards down the hall at Major Cole's office.

"Leaving, Major. It's been real, sir," Shawn announced with a smile as he extended a hand.

"Good to have worked with you, Shawn. I still think you should have been allowed to stay in the states after your help in that operation. But, you know, for the Afghan situation… We needed everyone back here that we could get. Everyone else is there now. I've enjoyed you being here with me."

"Oh, I know, Major. It wasn't your decision. It worked out fine, anyway. I've appreciated your leadership, sir."

"I know I never told you, Shawn, so I'll say it now. It *was* really serious. They had a dirty bomb ready to go. For that attack, you know? It was the real deal. You really did help save our asses…You should know that, son. It would have been a mess. They'd of killed thousands of soldiers and civilians *again*."

"Well, sir, if I had known it was an attack, I guess I would have felt more important."

"What are your plans when you get back, Shawn?"

"Amy and I are going to take our new daughter down to the Keys for a vacation. I'm anxious to use our new motorhome for the first time. I haven't seen it, yet, either. Amy picked it out. Then I'll get back to teaching, I think."

"No more snowmobiling?"

"Well, not for this year, sir… Maybe next. As much as I like it, there are other things to do, now. Especially with my daughter, you know."

"I understand, Shawn, I understand. And thanks again. It's been nice working with you, son, here *and* at home. Glad you made it through everything okay. My best to your wife, too."

"Thank you, my pleasure, sir," Shawn saluted. "See ya. And good luck on the rest of your tour."

"You bet… Thanks," the Major returned Shawn's salute.

"Corporal?" Shawn said as he nodded down the hallway.

"Yes, sir," he picked up the duffle quickly.

When he got into the Hum-Vee, a group of little kids ran up looking for candy. As always, Shawn had some for them and tossed it into their grubby outstretched hands.

Shawn managed to say, "Good luck, kids," but then his eyes welled up and he started to choke up before he could add take care and good-bye.

He looked forward and pointed for the Corporal to put his duffel in the vehicle. They drove rapidly out of the compound onto the dusty streets.

They wound their way quickly from the Green Zone out onto the "Highway of Death" toward Baghdad Airport. Shawn had been up and down that stretch hundreds of times, but this was the last trip and all his senses were extremely acute. In the back of his mind he was expecting the dreadful, the unexpected... the IED. Maybe it was having a child that made him more concerned. He had real responsibilities now. And maybe, since he and Amy reconciled their differences, things would go more smoothly at home. He wanted to be sure he arrived to help make it happen.

On the way to the airport he made an extra effort to salute, or nod, or give a thumbs-up to any military personnel that looked his way. He knew they all knew he was going home. Those leaving usually were in an upbeat mood that made a subliminal statement to the ones staying behind. It felt a little like the last day of college to Shawn, only better. Much better.

At the airport he saluted and thanked the Corporal and pulled his duffle from the Hum-Vee.

"Take care of yourself, Corporal. And those little guys back there. They're the future of this place and maybe us, too, you know?"

"Don't worry, I will, sir. And good luck to you, sir," he saluted with a smile.

Shawn made his way through the check points and onto the plane and settled into his window seat. He stared out of the window. He thought about what the future might hold for the people of this war-torn country. He wondered about those poor kids hanging around the compound and what would help them look more favorably at the occupation of their homeland. He wondered what his daughter looked like in real life, not just pictures on the computer. Would she eventually look a lot like these kids? Dark eyes, olive skin, black curly hair. Would she ever meet any of the children of Iraq? Would she even care to? He would make sure she knew what they were like, and he would be certain, when she was old enough to understand, to explain what they went through when he was here. Other than that, well, it's another country in a very different world.

The plane taxied out and took off without incident; never a certainty in Iraq.

No one sat in the middle seat but the passenger on the aisle was a Major-General about fifty years old. He was very well decorated and also leaving Iraq for good.

"Captain," he said and nodded to Shawn.

"Sir," Shawn replied with a salute.

"Headed home, son?" he asked.

"Yes. You, sir?"

"Yep, put in long enough here. Long enough for you, Captain?"

"Yes, sir. Had to come back after I thought I was through, sir. But it worked out fine."

"Oh, yeah?" After a brief pause, "Oh, the surge?"

"Ah, kind of, sir. But mainly we had a sting assignment back home, sir."

He looked over at Shawn's ID badge.

"Oh, okay…yeah, then. You're Kaan. You're that soldier that got hurt on an ATV chasing terrorists back in the states. I've heard about you, son. Some job there, Captain."

"Well, sir, it was a snowmobile. And actually *they* were chasing *me*… and my wife."

"Either way, son. I heard they were into some very bad stuff. That was my base they were going to strike; Fort Drum, you know ? Glad you helped stop them in any case. Did you get awarded? Don't see many medals there…You get your medals, son?"

"Ah…No, sir. But I *was* promoted to Captain."

"Well, what the hell? What? No medals?"

"As I understand it, sir, the White House and Homeland Security didn't want too many people to know exactly how far they got. Wouldn't look good to the average Joe if they knew it almost happened. I guess they didn't want a big public thing made of it."

"I suppose… Suppose, maybe… But we've given commendations to a lot less deserving soldiers than yourself. It's why we have these things," flicking at one of his many medals with his right thumb. He paused, thinking. "It'll happen yet, son. I'll *make* it happen. You'll see. That's just not right. I have some very good contacts. You'll see, we'll take care of *that*."

Shawn said, "Yes, sir. Thank you, sir. Whatever you think is right, sir."

"Yes, son…No problem. That *was* Fort Drum, correct? And Kaan, correct?"

"Yes, sir, it was… And, ah, yes, I am sir."

"Hmm, wow," he shook his head slowly then took out a booklet on retirement hotspots in the south and started to quietly read.

Shawn thought it might help Amy feel better if he *was* awarded a medal for their part in the successful sting operation. Although she was a very patriotic woman, she believed with all they went through, at least Shawn should get some recognition. After all, they were almost killed. Of course she could not complain about the medical care they were provided afterward. The Army took care of absolutely everything. It was the feeling of being used and then more or less forgotten or discarded that continued to nag at her.

As for Shawn, while he would not turn down a medal, he remained stoic about the whole ordeal. He allowed for any countries' military to view their soldiers basically as pawns. After all, who calls the shots? Not the enlisted men and women. Those who are probably going to get hurt, or in fact die, traditionally have had the least to say about it. Shawn knew it had been that way since armies were contrived and will probably stay that way forever.

He looked out his window at the blanket of puffy white clouds now far below them and thought of the snow drifts that he and Amy passed through in that monumental blizzard before the chase. It seemed so long ago. He wondered if they would ever get back to riding or if, after raising their child, they would have stopped for so long they would have lost all interest. Others they had known had quit and they didn't seem to miss it.

He would have to see. Maybe if they could get Shawna to ride early they could buy a big two-up—like Chuck Wagon's—and pack all three of them on it. It wouldn't be as much fun as riding by himself, and Amy would almost certainly have a fit riding two-up again, but Shawna would like it, he thought.

Yes, then, that's the plan. One big sled—one small, happy family.

Several hours into the flight, after listening to the engines make some strange noises, Shawn finally closed his eyes and drifted into a deep sleep…

… Shawn attempted to nip the apex of the ice-encrusted bend with his wife Amy, and daughter, Shawna aboard, laughing and hanging on for dear life!